QUINTET

Peter Abbot

Rock's Mills Press
Oakville, Ontario
2020

Published by
ROCK'S MILLS PRESS
www.rocksmillspress.com

For information, please contact the publisher at
customer.service@rocksmillspress.com.

… the deadly pestilence … started in the East … and it killed an infinite number of people…. Without pause it spread from one place and it stretched its miserable length over the West. And against this pestilence no human wisdom or foresight was of any avail … not only did talking to or being around the sick bring infection and a common death, but also touching the clothes of the sick or anything touched or used by them …

There were some people who … gathered in small groups and lived entirely apart … spending their time with music and other pleasures….

—Giovanni Boccaccio (1313–1375), *The Decameron*

ONE

Tuesday 31st March 2020
BORIS

Even the date seems like an ending. (End of WINTER!) But it's also a BEGINNING! (Beginning of SPRING!)

For several weeks now (how many? I'm already forgetting, and I guess that's not only my advanced age, 84, asserting itself, it's probably true of most of us, here in Canada, in my generation – we will be another Lost Generation and deserve to be, though I pray we don't take succeeding generations down with us – or maybe I do pray for that, for the end of Humanity - when I am able to believe, very temporarily and against all evidence, in the existence of God? A God who CARES – not merely atoms -)

And you see already, you who are reading this, that I am a confused old man. Gerontion? So why read what I write? (Don't BOTHER if you have something better to do!) (Actually I know I'm writing this for MYSELF alone – killing Time while waiting for DEATH? – though of course I know well enough that we don't ever kill Time, Time kills US, always has, always will!) (Did we Humans, we endlessly reproducing Humans, generally have a Good Time? Until it became a very Bad Time?) No doubt I am all too representative of the pullulating millions who have for so long been wrecking this planet. (I told them how it had to end!) It'll be like reading yourself out. (What does that mean?) Music is preferable, always has been. (Which is why I'm half-listening to a CD – Schubert's 'Unfinished Symphony' – Ha! Schubert, Schubert, if we can't perform your great Quintet – well, I'll play it again, later, again and again! My favourite CD. And your music CAN never finish – never!) (Oh – until WE do.) And if WE survive, our Lark Quartet-plus-One will perform that greatest-masterpiece with fervor, with gratitude, with JOY. With or without an audience. But definitely with its Founding Cellist! Yes, at least I am that! WOT LARKS!!!

JENNIFER - we were so glad to welcome her at the run-through of the Quintet - when we were expecting to perform it quite soon afterwards. Then, of course, the Plague burst upon us and is changing everything, EVERYTHING! We were forced to cancel the performance, as we all know. But I am living with the hope that we still may be able to rehearse and perform that glorious masterpiece one day! So – I was also about to tell her, Jennifer, and will, that we have a new custom (!), of sending emails to each other, to keep in touch – all of the members to send me a copy of their emails, when we are rehearsing or performing, and I will choose one every day and send it to all of you – This started as a JOKE but then I realized it was useful, we are a very close little musical group, as you'll discover, and it will be not only a good way to keep in touch and get to know each other, as a close group of musical builders rearing our "PALACE OF MUSIC"!!! We will try to be completely open with each other, no shame, no concealment – naked and unashamed! "Sorrow is hard to bear, and doubt is slow to clear … / But God has a few of us whom he whispers in the ear; / The rest may reason and welcome: 'tis we musicians know."

For several weeks (as I was saying before, as I HAVE said, haven't I?) that Plague named COVID-19 (or Coronavirus? – which is it? or has that ceased to matter? What's in a name? – Names change, a rose by any other name – etc – BUT this aint no rose! – NO, NO - THIS Plague is ravaging our planet. *Our* planet? We fucked you up, Earth. You were never OURS, but we used you as if we owned you, we ABused you! and now -) Yes – this Plague, this Pestilence, now destroying many many MANY human-beings, MILLIONS? in many many countries, starting in China, where it all began anyway, a few months ago – (China, where a few million citizens won't be missed? But would ANY of us be missed? After a few years?) Yes, where it all began, just a few months ago, in China, yes, as this joyful New Year of 2020 was also just beginning –

And I am an old man, as I was just saying - wasn't I? (84!) – and old people are apparently its preferred (COVIDED!) victims (yes, because the most CULPABLE, and most HELPLESS?) - so many of us dying now in our so-called seniors' homes – Definitely a majority of victims are Seniors, they say - OLD PEOPLE like me - most of us likely to die anyway before long, as a natural consequence of hosting several diseases that are (even as I type this!) feeding on our bodies – and our minds too, yes, CANCER and the dreaded ALZHEIMER'S above all.

Sorry, I am rampaging again!

She's calling me – Alice, I mean – calling me for supper. So, get up, old man, OLD MAN! – time to totter carefully, slowly, so SLOWLY, downstairs. Before she has to shout again. You are one of the fortunate ones, Boris! (And she's a good cook.) But think of all those in old-folks' homes ('seniors' homes' I should say) – think of how imprisoned they must be feeling – I really must telephone Archie tomorrow morning. (I did try, and failed, this morning.)

So, to each of you fellow members of a great Quartet, I have set you an example of UTTER OPENNESS!! Your turn now!

Wednesday 1st April 2020
JAMES

Another day without Ken. Stupid! – you *were* stupid, James. Why get so angry over such a small disagreement? And where is he now? I guess he'll want to punish me – but it's dangerous now, none of us can ignore the danger. Ken! Please don't be getting drunk in a bar. Please come back – or at least phone or email me, please, please –

But I'm talking to myself. I'll email the others maybe, the Four I mean. Jennifer & I would have gotten to know each other by now – the extra cellist – but we didn't get beyond our first run-through before the Govt began closing almost everything down – a few weeks ago, how fast the time goes! I guess that was necessary, most people seem to think so – governments in most countries are doing it -

I'm feeling like a prisoner – well, I guess most of the popula-tion of this city feel that way. And citizens all round the world! How easily & casually we just went about our lives, working in our offices during the day, visiting friends in the evening, restau-rants, pubs, watching TV or going to a show – Of course all the shows are cancelled now, & all sporting events, even the Olym-pics. Never thought I'd miss the Office – though problems accu-mulated there – & many angry clients - once the airlines started cancelling flights, & of course the cruise-ships, I think some of them are still stuck out at sea with a load of sick passengers & others who aren't & just want to be home – looks as if the whole Cruise industry is dead already, or dying – maybe even other travelling won't happen much in future & then what will I -?

In yesterday's local newspaper: "We're in a race against time" (headline) & "COVID-19 continues to spread as new travel restrictions imposed" (by Govt). April Fool's Day! For us all. Believe nothing, go back to sleep & dream happy dreams, you Fool!

Why do I go on rambling like this? An old habit – does it actually help to record disordered thoughts & feelings? - & then not even to look again, ever, at what I wasted time writing! Words, words! But it's deeds that matter now - & music, the soul needs music, & not only the soul - my brain, my emotions, even my muscles are twitching – That concert, yes of course it was cancelled, like everything else, weeks ago, & I was specially looking forward to it. The Schubert Quintet in C! My Mother loved it, *loved* it, & so do I, I always did – it's partly why I chose to learn the violin! & so does – oh Ken. Please.

So I'll send out another of my urgent emails – "KEN, I LOVE YOU, PLEASE COME HOME". (Boris, *are* you *reading* this? Are any of you?) (*Your* crazy idea, Boris!) (So now, pay attention!)

I wonder if this will work? This scheme that Boris has imposed on us, on all the members of the Quartet. Seems crazy, as I say! And on No. 5 as well, the second cello. Jennifer – are you reading this? You're only temporary of course, just for the Schubert Quintet that we were scheduled to perform before the Pandemic shut everything down. But Boris insists that we *will* perform the Quintet this summer! Crazy! Why the insistence, Boris? And that we each send him a daily diary-entry from now on, & he will choose one to represent each day, & they will accumulate into a record of our lives as we rehearse. Crazy idea! But you were always crazy, Boris. *You* said that! So you can choose me to represent today – after all, it's April Fool's Day, & I'm the Fool – so, as they say, ENJOY! Enjoy my discomfort, my pain, all of you. Laugh at me! My turn will come! (If you play fair, Sir!) (Remember, you said "Totally honest & open!")

Thursday 2nd April 2020
ANNA

What a glorious day! Well, it's not, of course, in the context of what we are all enduring, this COVID-19 PANDEMIC that's terrifying us all; but it is, otherwise, so gloriously bright and sunny that you just long to be out there in the Park! When I went out onto the balcony for a few minutes, with my coffee, just very briefly, I could see only one moving figure on the Park path, a young man in shorts (in SHORTS!) running along the main path. Otherwise hardly any movement, even along the street: only two cars, and nobody, NOBODY, walking along the sidewalk. You feel as if you're on the moon!

Myrna, are you there? Still in bed? Surely not.

Main headline in today's newspaper: "Surge anticipated in next three weeks". Surge of what? COVID-19 patients, what else? And helpful articles about local education, like "Now is the time to focus on what really matters – not the school year"! I wonder about all my kids. Some of them will be doing the work I put on the website, especially if their Mothers push them, like that Mrs. Cohen; but the immigrant kids, or the two refugee kids; and I wonder what their parents are doing, if they still have jobs? Well, I can't help there, can I? But I'll try to call the School after breakfast and find out what's happening. It's good that Trudeau and the Government are doing something about the economy: apparently so many Canadians are in financial difficulty, not being able to pay their rent this month or whatever. Worrying; what a mess!

I read an article somewhere, the other day, about keeping a diary: how helpful to be doing that in this period when CO-VID-19 is making us stay indoors. So it's good that I have always kept one! And especially now that Boris has again demanded that we forward each entry to him. Why? But I could hardly refuse! (Well, I will refuse if you are just playing a game with us, Sir!)

Friday 3rd April 2020
JENNY

I'm surprised that the newspaper is still being delivered. I must try to thank the newsboy – if I talk to him from this side of the front-door, surely I would be far enough away, but maybe I shouldn't give him a tip – they say that type of physical contact could transmit the virus or whatever it is – but at least I could say Thank You at arm's length, surely? I wonder when he delivers the newspaper? Probably too early for me to get to the front-door, maybe I should pin a thank-you note to the screen-door? But if he stops delivery, I wouldn't really miss it - the CBC News on the radio is enough, *more* than enough, these days, I think! In fact, there's a *lot* of things that clutter one's life which, I confess, I wouldn't really miss.

But what a shock when I did read the newspaper – I saw the main headline, "We're in a race against time", so then I read, in the end, almost everything there – and as I say, what a shock to see how the whole COVID-19 situation, here in Hamilton, is much *much* more serious than I knew. I must call Sheila tonight in case they don't know up there in Cottage Country! An article on the front page is entitled "COVID-19 continues to spread as new travel restrictions imposed" and in the article it says "Ontario reported its largest single-day increase by far … 351 new COVID-19 cases and ten more deaths Monday, the province's largest single-day increase by far, as Premier Doug Ford warned that a shortage of critical medical supplies may be perilously close…" That disturbed me all day on and off – I could hardly concentrate on what I was reading - and then on TV in the evening, the news under the screen had this: "80K COVID-19 CASES IN ONT. BY APRIL 30" - and in the American news in the CBC newscast, "Trump orders US Company to stop exporting masks to Canada" – just when it seems wearing a mask - I haven't got one - is likely to become mandatory even in the super-market. As I say, all a shock to me, and no doubt to many Canadians.

And it's a real pity about the Schubert Quintet, I was really looking forward to that – the rehearsals and the three performances - they're such a good Quartet, one of the best, otherwise they wouldn't be in such demand to go on tours in Europe as well as Canada. I was lucky to be invited because they needed an extra cello for the Schubert – which I love! It was Anna who arranged the invitation, I think - she has played Second Violin in the Quartet for quite a few years, and I know that Boris, who started it after he came to Canada with his parents, all those years ago – they were refugees, I think – has said how much he admires her playing, he told me that - I had a sort of interview with him, he's an old man and he did make some strange comments, I thought – Anna said he had been a refugee from I think she said Hungary and came to Canada as a boy or young man, with his parents who had been members of a major orchestra. He has a strong accent! But I had no problem understanding him. He's tough, I think, and of course he has very high standards. I played movements from Bach, the third cello suite, which I have always loved, and he grunted and said I'd "do". (Hope I haven't offended you, Sir, by writing down my thoughts just as they were – but you did say to write down honestly whatever I was thinking! So that's what I'm doing!)

(Also, it's good in a way, I think, that I have time now, with this shut-in situation we're all in, to write down things I would otherwise forget!)

Saturday 4th April 2020
KEN

You there, James? Were you wondering about me – what I did, where I went, after I walked out on April Fool's Day? See, you don't know much about me, do you? I always said that, didn't I? I always came way down at the bottom of your attention. Your interest. I always said that. I'm BORING! You never paid attention and I doubt if you will now. Anyway, I'm coming back later today. It's *my* apartment, or *was*, wasn't it? I PAY THE RENT. You are MY GUEST, and anyway you only care about playing your bloody fiddle! I mean, apart from making-out with any passing Bunny. Oh and the World of Travel. You were into Cruises and now all that might be gone – so many cruise-ships and their contents stuck out at sea because no port wants to let their passengers on land distributing a plague! Surprise! So who will risk going on a cruise in future? – Oh well, doesn't matter. YOU don't matter. And obviously I DON'T MATTER to you!

Just useful that my apartment is in the Village. "So convenient" you said. Well, it is – but remember, I pay the rent. You have your own place – remember?

Dan – Remember him? You sneered that I let him pick me up in the Workhorse. Well, that's who I've been with for a week. Other side of TO. Better believe it! We've had a real good time together. Said he wants me to come back and live permanently with him! He has to go and see about his Father first. Who's in a Home, I think I told you that. But now the Home is closing – four deaths from that COVID or whatever-it's-called. So they emailed him. The Home has to close down! Dan says he thinks his cousin will look after him, but if not he will have to bring him back here.

So that's how things are. Dan will be leaving soon. He's going by train, if it's operating, and if it isn't he'll have to go by bus. He's trying to find out right now, but they aren't answering. Just a message to try again later, he says. I'll be leaving when he does. With a suitable gap between us, of course. He has a reputation to protect! Unlike feckless musicians, banker-types must dress well and behave better!

I've been reading the newspaper while I'm waiting. Shock! It says, I'm quoting, "Canada's most populous province" that's us of course "could see between 3,000 to 15,000 deaths because of COVID, according to predictions from Ontario public health officials." *15,000!* And the Mayor said that *over 1,600 could be dead by the end of this month!* "That is 50 a day or that is two people every hour." Wow. Think about that! Yet some people are still getting together in big groups, for parties, even when it's against the law now. I've seen that, really stupid behaviour! People are getting nervous and officious. Yesterday when I went for a walk, someone shouted at me, bloody fool! - but you got to get SOME exercise. I'm already – Hope the buses are still running. If not, you may not see me ever again! EVER!!!

Anyway, here's Dan. Says he's ordered a taxi and it can take me home after it drops him off at the station. So I'll send this to you now. So I'll see you soon. And I hope you will have read this by then and will be ready for me. My great Comeback!

TWO

Sunday 5th April 2020
JENNY

What a glorious day! How I would have enjoyed a walk in the Park and by the Lake! The dog along the street has been barking again - I hope it's not imprisoned indoors, like the one that was kept in next-door's basement through most of last year – I can't bear cruelty to animals!

But I'm rambling, Anna. Sorry. It was good to have that chat last night & know that we are both still alive! I'm so glad I decided to telephone – though I wondered if that was allowed. So many things we aren't allowed to do now – or *must* do, like washing & washing & *washing* one's hands. It reminds me of being a schoolgirl in England again! And I wonder how the kids I teach, taught, will manage! I must try to talk to all of them today on my iphone & see how they are getting on. Poor kids! But they'll have to get used to it. This could be their Future! How do you feel about it? Same as me? I wonder if they'll be more rambunctious when this is all over? If it ever is! Or quieter, calmer?

Anna, did you listen to the Queen's Address this afternoon? It was on CBC TV. Very inspiring. I should have mentioned it when we talked last night. She's 93! Even older than Boris!! Didn't he say he's 83? – when he was congratulating himself, at that first & so-far-only read-through Schubert rehearsal? Queenie quoted Vera Lynn, "We'll meet again." "Don't know where, don't know when"! My Mother used to sing that. She was a child during the War, in England. She was a Vackie, sent to the Midlands somewhere, a farm, she hated that, but she also said it probably saved her life. My Dad, he was much older than her, & he fought in North Africa, but he wouldn't ever talk about that, or anything about the War, "Better forgotten" he'd say. Sorry, I'm rambling. I was telling you about the Queen's Address. She also said "Better days will return" & "We will succeed". Of course it's her job to cheer us up! They even showed a clip of her & her little sister Princess Margaret giving a talk during the War, cheering up other children of England & the Empire. But I should also say that, before the Queen came on, the CBC said that 5,000 people have already died of what's-it, COVID-19, *already*, in the U.K. Which is frightening, isn't it?

It was such a lovely morning, & I was just longing to go out walking!

You asked me if I'd like to be in England now, & I said I'd think about it. No, I don't think so. Did I tell you I'm an only child? And both my parents died some time ago, my mother was killed when I was a small girl, she was knocked down by a speeding car, it was terrible, I can't really talk about it, I don't want to think about it. And my father, he fell to pieces, so I was brought up by my aunt, & the only good thing was that she was a cellist, quite a famous cellist really, & she taught me – Aunt Emily, she was a lovely kind person, & a teacher, so I suppose that's why I am a teacher – & a cellist, I love the cello, you know that. But I *despise* the violin, such a thin screechy sound! Oh, I'm teasing you, Anna! Boris said to write freely, just what we are feeling, so blame him when I insult you!!!

I wish we could get together. We're both lonely, aren't we? Or at least *I* am.

Monday 6th April 2020
BORIS

News that the British Prime Minister who has had COVID for a while is now in Special Care, is that what they call it? In a London hospital. I wonder how seriously ill he is? Anyway, he'll get the best care possible, so if he doesn't make it, gloom will definitely spread through the UK. Maybe won't be much better over here – in New York, latest news very serious! Trump has jumped again, from denying that they have a problem, to saying Yes, they do have a problem, but of course he is on TOP of it, he will SAVE AMERICA!!!! – but of course, and everyone knows this except for his Supporters, he will just claim that he was right, whatever situation develops! The TRUTH means nothing to him – as we all know now.

But why bother with Trump? Alice, where art thou? Your ancient decrepit husband needs FOOD! Before he settles into his after-lunch nap. (I wonder if the Queen takes a nap? She's a real trooper, that was a great speech she gave on TV yesterday! She was calm, consoling, helpful, even *hopeful*. I think a lot of her audience would have been as impressed as I was! Of course she would be protected from any chance of that virus getting into HER system, but she wasn't always so protected - especially during the War, I think, or when she went travelling in other countries.) And look at what we've heard on this evening's news, that the British Prime Minister is in Hospital now, with that CO-VID-19! Will he survive? If he doesn't, could be a panic in the whole population of England!! Tense days!

Ah, I hear Alice. Soon she'll appear with my dinner. I don't feel very hungry but I should eat. (In my earlier, conducting days, I was a big eater - and DISCRIMINATING, all those superb restaurants, when I was First Cello in the LSO, that was the life!!!) And then Alice, I should have avoided romance, she wasn't even a very good pianist – but she offered to accompany me, when I needed to prepare, and that was It!! Sometimes I've thought that she trapped me into marriage - and then didn't even produce children! But she looks after me now, we are two old friends heading for the Exit, hand in hand! (Are you reading this, my dear? Of course not, you are not a Member of the Quartet. So am I talking to myself! And I haven't been the best husband, have I? Or have I?) (Dear Readers, do not be shocked by my levity. Alice knows, I hope, that I love her.)

Now I'm back for a final contribution to today's record. After my after-lunch snooze. (Who will read it when I'm gone, or even value it? My journal. I thought of leaving it to the National Gallery or, if they don't want it – they didn't want the diary of a fine composer I knew! – to a University Collection. DIARY OF A MUSICAL GENIUS WHO WAS ALSO A WAR-REFUGEE!!!! But now, even if we survive, and even if the survivors value classical music – who knows? This record, of our thoughts and activities might be - And I am contradicting myself, I think. Who was it said "If I wish to contradict myself, I'll contradict myself!" (NOT Trump, long before him, but same type of human-being!) As Alice once said, woundingly, keeping a diary is just your little time-wasting hobby. That did hurt, my dear – you knew it would hurt!)

Our newspaper's main headline: "Outbreak at retirement home escalates" – "Thirteen residents and five staff … have COVID-19". And another front-page article: "Ontario COVID-19 deaths jump past 100". Hard not to be depressed. And on TV, a discussion about how demanding and depressing, and dangerous, daily work is for the doctors and nurses who tend hospital patients. They also need more surgical masks, and apparently our great noble friendly neighbour to the South has stopped them being sent here, they are only for REPUBLICAN AMERICANS?

That young cellist, who Anna recommended as second cellist, for the Schubert, telephoned me last night, apparently for a chat. Alice told me she's probably frightened and needed a shoulder to cry on – well, maybe she did, and I did talk to her for a while, but I hope she won't make a habit of this. It was Anna who brought her in, and she *is* quite a good cellist, I agree. But I am NOT a good SUGAR-DADDY, having had no practice, that's what I told Alice – who clearly thought I was somehow criticizing *her*! Oh well, time for bed. I wonder if these diary-bits *are* a good idea? Maybe, like that email stuff the young do, they encourage one to throw aside barriers of politeness and honesty. (Or so I hope!!!)

I can still pray, I find, even though my prayers have no recipient.

"Gentle Jesus, meek & mild"? But your bad Daddy has it in for us! "The Lord is my shepherd …" Yes, and we are Your sheep!

Tuesday 7th April 2020
KEN

So I'm back! Not that my Beloved seems to care – are you listening, Jimmy-boy? But I know who *is* listening, while he lies there, basking in our total subservience, our love, love, love – he will even purr while plotting evil against us, won't you? – (No, not you, dear Boris!) Oh Pusska, almighty Pusska, if you harbor this disease that's killing us humans, please accept our total submission and remember where your milk and sustenance come from. Besides, we adore you, as I was saying. Surely it's only Tigers, like that one in the news, who fall victim to COVID-19. Among animals, I mean. And they are far away, in India or zoos.

Oh, James, I am so BORED already. Maybe I need to run off again. James, are you listening? You may be First Violin, but Schubert loved the viola. *Loved* it! He was *passionate* about the viola, you can hear that – the recording that Boris sent each of us, which may not be the *perfect* interpretation of the Quintet, tells us that our lovely Schubert, whatever his other fancies and proclivities, and apparently he was a very good boy, though how did he get syphilis, then? – but he loved the VIOLA. And *I* love the viola. And if you ever again cast aspersions on it, even in a joke, my dear old James, I will smash your effete instrument, your commonplace little violin, into a million fragments!

And I don't think you even bother to read my emails, do you? If you do – well, you don't. (But Other People will!)

And I don't think, to be completely honest, that I can settle to reading any of those Jane Austens you keep on recommending. Shakespeare? Maybe – one of the comedies? But not now, not today.

So. I'll do my washing. I'll read the newspaper (must keep up with the news – all about COVID, as if nothing else was happening, *anywhere*). Oh, there's the British PM, fighting for his life, as they say, even if he is just lying there, unable to speak or think, poor man. He may have been the Ultimate Bastard, ruining his country by pulling it out of Europe – but as PM he is clearly extra-precious now and far above the lives and feelings of his subjects, let them eat cake! Am I merely mean – as you once said, do you recall that quarrel? – when we first started being together? You said I had no feelings!

It's a grey day today – "disconsolate" is the word that comes to my mind. And still a bit cool. I went out onto the balcony for a short while, just to get some fresh (?) air – hardly any traffic, the odd car or bus, or police cruiser – but, over in the park, that madman, running, running - in shorts!!! Nothing stops him. Or ever will. Except (whisper it) Death.

4:30. Yes, Death is now our neighbor. Maybe one day,

quite soon, we will be able to laugh, or at least smile, remembering our fears. Or maybe not. Tonight on CBC I notice that the final appearance of *Schitt's Creek* is scheduled; I intend to watch (you too?), I never had more than a glimpse of it earlier (too busy? No, just never connected), but apparently it's been a worldwide success, so one ought to bow down & worship. I'm not really joking – Trumptrash has just been trampling us again, I'm sure you noticed, ordering a company that makes Masks to cease fulfilling any Canadian orders, so – Apparently that's over now, that skirmish, though there will be more – why does he hate Trudeau? Because he's young and pretty? Or because we're too weak up here to matter? When he has those Dictator friends –

Oh, James, please let's not connect only thisaway – it's time to forgive me, your Peppy Playboy, you once called me that, remember? – So *please!* See, I'm begging – I who, I mean whom, you also once called Ultimate Snob. (I'm *not* a snob!) We can't go on like this – & especially *now* when the world's falling apart & we are all threatened. Wonder if our dear Schubert felt like this when he knew his time was going, going – but, before it was gone, the glory of that Quintet!!! – we *must* play it, if only as our apotheosis. And *then*, Master Death, you can take us. James, WE ARE FRIENDS!!! Remember?

Wednesday 8th April 2020
ANNA

Another grey day! What are you up to, my dear Second Cellist? Something more noble than washing your smalls, I hope; or making a list for a quick shop, for basic survival requirements like bread and milk. I'm already getting edgy. Did I tell you that I once had a stay in hospital with extreme depression, when I was a university student. I hated it; in fact that reaction is what ultimately saved me, I think - hating it. All I wanted was to get out of there, and I had enough sense left to see that only obedience and smiles would accomplish thhat! So I became a failed nurse, and then a music-teacher! Teaching kids to love Schubert (I hope)!

You said you were lonely, Jenny? Wonder if we could get together, if only for a short while? But no doubt that is *verboten* too. There was a list on the radio, CBC, this morning, of things one *mustn't do*, but I didn't listen carefully. Did you? Please email me back anyway! And I will call you this evening, it was lovely to hear your voice and to have that conversation. We're lucky these days to have both the telephone, for chats, and also the iphone etc. I tell that to my kids, warning them about the internet and to be careful what they write in emails; though I guess you can also be recorded on the telephone? So just be careful about what you say, which is good anyway! They are undisciplined!

Sorry, I'm just rambling. Did you watch "Schitt's Creek" last night? A lot of self-congratulating went on. I shouldn't really have wasted my time, except that one has so much time to waste now! And I was tired of reading. But something I saw in this morning's newspaper (I wonder how long that will continue now, delivery of the paper I mean) was that Bill Withers has died. He was 81, almost as old as Boris, but he had retired long ago, Bill Withers; you may not have heard of him, but you may have heard a song of his, I loved it, I can hear him in my memory, his lovely warm voice, singing it: "Lean on Me", do you know it? When I was – I just told you about my depression when I was a student, maybe I was thinking about that, I mean because of that item about Bill Withers dying. I loved that song, and I had it on a tape that I would play and play until it wore out. Oh, sorry, Jenny, I guess I'm just – but I'm being self-indulgent and unfair to you. What else? I'm reading a lovely novel. I'll tell you about it later, when I've finished it.

Did you notice in yesterday's newspaper - ? Maybe you don't get it. There was a long article on the cholera epidemic in Hamilton, in 1854. It said that at least 550 people died, out of the city's population of less than 20,000; and that was after an earlier epidemic, in 1832, that was "also disastrous". The newspaper also reported that the number of Americans who have died so far in our COVID-19 has now reached 12,000, with 350,000 confirmed infections. But yesterday the paper said "COVID-19 DEATHS LEVEL OFF IN NEW YORK". A massive number of protective masks now in use or on order, but "medical masks are in short supply" and we are being urged to make our own masks, to wear when we go shopping! Why do I keep noting facts and figures?

Well, they do concern the survival of our fellow human-beings, and include us truly, though I must say that just trying to think about all of this is truly mind-stretching and depressing. I wonder if any experts are now saying or thinking "Over-population" But then what difference would that make - in a situation when, clearly, the world's population might be decimated? Would the disappearance of humans be beneficial for all other creatures? I never asked you – are you religious? Do you go to church?

I am not good at thinking out things, Jenny. I think you are better at that. Maybe it helps being younger. You probably guessed, from my grey hair, I am in my fifties, and semi-retired. Just an old school-marm! You'd probably not like to talk about teaching; especially now. But we both love music!

I'll telephone you for a chat this evening. If you don't want that, just tell me. I won't be offended! If only we could get together. We could play duets? My piano's in tune. Or we could listen to some of my CDs; and I could offer tea and cookies etc! By the way, I think Boris gave all of us copies of that CD of the Schubert String Quintet, as performed by the Weller Quartet? I hope you have it too? A good performance, he told me. "Listen carefully to that! But *we* can do better!" The two of us - We could listen to it, and play our parts, as practice, with it. And I have other CDs that you might enjoy; we could listen together.

I'll sign off now, Jenny. Would you mind if I call you Jennifer? I feel more comfortable with full names. I have the CBC News on, I was half-listening to that wonderful Organ Symphony by Saint Saens (have I spelt that right?); but then the News came on and they have just said that the number of COVID deaths in England today is almost one thousand! And their Prime Minister is still in hospital with that disease. And how many more deaths have occurred in Ontario and the rest of Canada? Oh, where will this end? So troubling – if only one could stop thinking about it! But it's wrecking our lives.

Thursday 9th April
JAMES
Oh, oh, oh, oh. Every morning the reports of COVID-19

deaths in Canada and of course around the world are worse. And it's Maundy Thursday today (do you know that, my dear Pagan?), a sunny windy day, Springlike, clearing away cobwebs and dust (Good Friday tomorrow – that will feel timely for Christians around the world, maybe? - & then Easter Sunday) - & 20,000 cases in Canada, 500 deaths, 2 million infected, 400,000 jobs lost in Ontario alone, & so on & so on … Awful, ugly facts accumulating. What are we going to do, Ken? Let's be very serious, very mature for once, and think it out together. No more fucking about. I am thinking that, for a start, you should come here so we can work things out together, live together permanently or semi-permanently. Then you won't be able to go on accusing me of trying to take over your apartment! This house is too big for me – I should never have inherited it – or I should have sold it immediately & bought myself a condo right in the Gay Village. And all possibility of daily work is gone, as you know – no cruises, no travelling abroad or even in Canada, & surely your mysterious travel & financial activities are gone too – aren't they? "Nevermore!" Cruise-ships are dead, & probably airlines too. (Oh, but maybe your Income Tax stuff? Time for that. But will it still happen? Nothing is as it was! But you have so many irons in your fire, so to speak! - No, take that how you like – no further comment! Trudeau will surely legislate a tax delay? I'm trying to be serious, and you should help me!)

Do you ever read Agony Aunt stuff? Me neither, but in this morning's paper, I guess because there was time to sit & read it through, this headline caught my eye: "Single, frightened amid global pandemic". And is that *me*? To be honest – maybe. I thought Maybe. Anyway, the letter started like this: "I'm 42, single, live alone & I'm scared." And I, Kenneth Blair, am 37, single, live alone, & - "I can't visit my parents because they're elderly and health-compromised, I can't visit my brother who lives out of town" & doesn't want to know anyway! And finally "I work, read, go out only for groceries & other essentials & eat alone. The news frightens me more every day…. I have no relationships at all now, & I'm not even sure why I'm writing this." So then I sat there, at the kitchen table, for a while, drinking coffee & reading the newspaper & thinking, and Pusska eventually jumped up onto me to ask if I was still alive. AM I still alive, Ken? Are YOU? How much longer have we got? Are we friends or enemies? And also my Mother, I think I told you she's frail, in a Home other side of Toronto, I haven't visited her, & maybe neither have my sister & brother, though they put her there - I haven't talked to them since they attacked me for being gay ten years ago, at my Father's funeral. But my Mother – how could I forget her, even if she betrayed me – as I said, I just haven't visited her, maybe she's already dead, maybe the Home she's in is one of those in the news, decimated by the virus? So – well, you see why I'm a mess? – All that, just from reading a letter to an agony-aunt! But, Ken. Let's talk. Really talk. Please. Maybe there's not much time left.

I should stop writing emails to you. We should talk. You should come & live with me. PLEASE TELEPHONE. I don't plan on going out tonight (!!!).

THREE

Friday 10th April 2020
BORIS

Sun and wind (*very* windy; I hear it whistling round this big old house, looking for a way in!). And it's Good Friday! I'm going to listen, yet again, to the CD of the Schubert Quintet (I've provided them all with that), it inspires and consoles me – but before that I'll listen to that Haydn Quartet, the one that superbly transmutes Christ's suffering into a series of variations. (Of course I'm not a Christian, but I do recognize the horror of tortures like that crucifixion.) And after that, yes, the Berlioz Requiem. Yes, however painful life can be, music transmutes it into calm beauty. Only music!

And that makes me think of Jennifer, Jenny, the Second Cellist, my Schubert companion. Who will often have to play in total unity with me. Since she emailed me, I've been thinking of her as being in a lonely, maybe frightening, situation, in crime-ridden Hamilton, in the basement of an empty house near the University (we have given quite a few concerts in the Great Hall there, over the years) and that she could come and live here! – and practice playing in total unity - In fact, occurs to me that this old house is big enough to accommodate all six of us – I must ask Alice about that, and whether we have enough beds & bedclothes etc (I could sleep at night in my wheelchair, or in an arm-chair, I've done that before – & if we worked out schedules etc - & then we could practise the Quintet, and play quartets – surely that will work?) - And *perform* the Quintet, as I have always longed to do! Listen together to glorious music – which would be a fine way of living through this period of enforced isolation, yes –

Who was it, which Classical story, where they all gathered together – yes, during a Plague – escaping the Plague - & told each other stories – *Decameron? Why* can't I remember? My memory – NOT Boccherini, I have played his cello sonatas, & I think a cello concerto, eighteenth-century composer – NOT Botticelli, medieval Italian artist, if I remember correctly – but -

NOW I have it, BOCCACCIO, they take refuge from the Black Death & pass the time telling stories, in Florence – yes, that's it -

But, speaking of favourite music, I've been listening to one of my old CDs (talking of quartets) which I always used to play on Good Friday – Haydn's set of "Crucifixion" Quartets, glorious music - & now I think I'll listen to the Berlioz Requiem – but haven't I already said that -?

Should I first record the day's news about the Virus? Well, maybe it will have some value for the Future, if there is one. Is that why I'm doing this? And recording our chats. For Posterity. So here goes. The latest official count of Canadian cases, 18,000; number of Canadians infected, 2 million; prediction of 23,000-to-32,000 cases of infection by mid-April, with 500 to 700 deaths; present job-loss in Ontario, 400,000. And the concern about murderous Plague infections in old-age homes is now joined by concern about the vulnerability of prisoners in jails – Will there be good social changes when this society gets back to normal, if it ever does? It seems doubtful – but maybe I'm just a habitual cynic. Yes , Alice, I am!

I have been thinking about past experiences – as far back as I can remember! Happy & painful memories. Mostly painful. Well, the War - But then music, to the rescue?

Saturday 11th April
ANNA

A call from Jennifer quite early this morning (I think we're probably all getting lazy, staying in bed longer than before – or maybe it's just me getting old and making excuses!). Anyway, after friendly enquiries - I think she is concerned about my ability to shop etc, but she needn't be, I'm still capable – she made what seemed to be a silly offer – that I should live with her in her flat - and I thought Why should she suggest that, when I'm living not far from her in a house that's too big for me, opposite the Park and close to the supermarket? - and then I realized she was actually meaning something different, that she's lonely and maybe scared, as so many people seem to be - and so half-suggesting or hoping that I would invite her to live with me while this Pandemic goes on. Yes, and maybe it would make sense in other ways, for companionship, and she could help with shopping etc, and I do have a spare bedroom!– and none of my family have visited for a good while. But I didn't say anything on those lines and in fact ended the conversation quite soon after that.

Also some questions arose in my mind as I began to think things out, while I was drinking coffee after breakfast. When and if everything goes back to normal, will my life go back to how it was? And even, would I want it to, because to be honest I do get lonely sometimes in this house; a bit like Boris, I used to think, and his house in TO is much bigger and older than mine. When I lived there, and of course I was much younger then, I used to find it demanding, keeping the house reasonably clean, while cooking for him and so on; and that almost became too much for me, with my teaching and studies, although I was much younger then of course; and that's why we had that row and I walked out; and Alice took my place, you could say, soon after, and then he married her. I should have detached myself completely after that, but then I still had my music, I *still* have my music and always will have – well, at least as long as the Lark Quartet survives, and my teaching; and also he eventually apologized; I think Alice made him do that, she and I are second-cousins – Oh, Anna! Stop this! Just stop it and think about that young woman, Jennifer, and what to do about her.

And the Coronavirus (COVID-19, I wish they'd stick to one name! why don't they?). It's beginning to take a toll on all of us, and our lives: warnings from local authorities of very big fines, even more than $500 I think, if you are in the company of more than one (related) person and if you are less than two yards from another person! something like that – it's getting crazy! Hard to remember all the figures of where it's at now, but I think about 100,000 global deaths, including 20,000 American, 10,000 in UK now, and it's beginning in Africa (where one must fear that the death total will be huge): so seems all this has a long way to go, with enormous suffering. But will it result in a significant reduction in the world's population? Other people must have wondered, like me, if the world's population will be much reduced ultimately? That's also an issue in relation to global-warming, or should be? Too many millions of us human-beings! The world shudders and recoils under us.

Enough for now. Thinking about that girl, though, makes me also think about the Schubert and other music. It would be lovely to be playing it right now, calming, glorious! And we could play together, she and I, violin and cello: Schubert, maybe some Haydn or Mozart or Beethoven – jolly old Haydn, he would be best!

Sunday 12th April – Easter Sunday!
JAMES

A bright breezy day! We may be incarcerated, but at least there are many activities to enjoy. I've just come back from a walk to the Park, & there, as well as on the way there and back, neighbours were exercising dogs and shouting greetings across the street to each other (wish I could have taken you with me, Pusska – but at least you have been able to relax subsequently on the back lawn under my surveillance!). And one beggar I know came right up to me & demanded money for his lunch – I quickly gave him some quarters & almost ran away! And there was a runner who waved as if I was a friend, but he didn't look familiar. I thought of Ken – as I often do! - & wished he was here, living with me rather than swimming in & out of my life. Maybe I'm just getting old & couldn't any longer function in the gay life of Church & Jarvis – well, I know I couldn't - though of course that has changed too since the days & nights of my wild youth. So long ago! I don't even want to try any of that now. Maybe I'm ready to settle down at last! – as Mom predicted I would, eventually, though I have always resisted.

But why am I spending Easter Day arguing with myself? It's up to Ken. And he's ten years younger than me – so why should he feel the pinch of Time Passing, the way I am? And surely I've shown him how much I care for him? We have so much in common. (Beyond chamber-music, Schubert's Quintet! Maybe.) Or is that perhaps part of the problem for him? But enough, James – enough.

I always turn on my bedside radio when I wake up, & on

Sundays there's Michael Enright's "Sunday Edition", which is often good value. It sure was good value this morning. (Oh I should first mention that our dear Queen has given another uplifting speech, a short one, urging love & kindness – & her controversial PM Boris Johnson has survived his bout of COVID-19 – these items just before, or was it after, the news that the UK coronavirus death-toll has now passed 1,000, with 9,000 infected - & we also learnt that in Canada the forecast is 23,000-to-32,000 cases, with 500-to-700 deaths, by mid-April, which is this week! Isn't it? And what else? Bill Gates, billionaire, is financing a search for a vaccine, "the only way forward", but it will likely be 18 months before it is available! And meanwhile? Better not to think about that? And a final item - today is the 200th birthday of Florence Nightingale!!! End of my little news-summary. And I think the end of my news-summarising altogether. Too depressing. And – "Everybody knows"! (Leonard Cohen) – or should do, or can do - every news outlet provides "fake- news"? – CBC TV advertises, non-stop, its commitment to informing us of the very latest "COVID-19 developments". It will exhaust our capacity to know or care! And so the end of this lengthy parenthesis.)

Back to "Sunday Edition" & forward to Enright's first item. Coventry Cathedral, bombed almost to total destruction by the Luftwaffe on Easter Day, 1940, but now restored, has a female Canadian Organist! called Rachel ?Mahon, lively & authoritative in discussing Canadian organ music (Healey Willan being the big name – English composer of English church-music). I enjoyed her interview, lively & knowledgeable – wish there had been more clips of her performing – As a young man, I was addicted to the organ (as to Christianity) - A choirboy in Toronto &, I should recall, a scholar at an Anglican Church school now notorious for the homosexual proclivities of its Masters (Yes, Ken, I'm glad you asked – yes, how could I have escaped? - of course I was a pretty & especially helpless potential victim) – but music saved me! I learned how to play the organ, had already fallen in love with the organ as a small boy, in the church services we were forced to attend in the School Chapel - & I was drawn also to the Organist & choir-master, a charming elderly man. Fatherly. (I told you about my actual father, you remember, what a bully he was, etc). A friend of his, to whom he introduced me, was a middle-aged cellist who had achieved a reputation across Canada & beyond. Yes, unless you are more stupid than I think, Ken (& you're not!), you've guessed it. Who he was. My future unfolded. I was not destroyed. I think.

Enough for now. You know, I've been thinking . Can't we use our emailing, not only to entertain & communicate with the other four, but also sight-read some quartets together & even rehearse the Schubert Quintet? I defer to your advanced technological know-how. But after my next email, I'll try to communicate with all the others apart from you & find out exactly what they think, & what's going on with them – Boris, Anna & Jenny – I guess we're all feeling apprehensive & bored & isolated.

But please reply to this one only to me – I didn't intend to, of course, but I *have* told you about myself in this email, things I wouldn't normally tell the others, & now I think it's your turn to be Confidential, Mr Viola, & let me into the darkest recesses of your being! After that, we'll both be completely open to the others. Right?

Monday 13th April
JENNY

Oh, oh, oh, oh. The CBC news this morning is still saturated with that Quebec nursing-home scandal. 31 deaths of Seniors (more than one for each day of this month!), in appalling circumstances of neglect - & of course it reflects a general situation, in seniors' homes across Canada, as Staff fall ill with COVID-19 & can't be replaced, & helpless seniors are left in isolation, with night-clothes & bed-clothes stinking-filthy. Oh, to think of that - & it does make me think of when Mum & Dad died, he had Alzheimer's & she had a bad fall when she was visiting him, before she was knocked down & killed – but at least they had good medical treatment, & things to do, & pleasant surroundings, & they were together in one room, & we could visit - & the Staff were kind, one even telephoned me to talk about them & suggest that I visit. But that was in England, a few years before I immigrated here. In all my hospital-volunteering, here in Ontario, when I was an undergraduate, and then in my brief abortive nursing career during the SARS epidemic, I never saw or heard of anything as bad as in that Report this morning.

Maybe I should see if I can volunteer or give some help in the Hospital. If I had moved in with Anna, she's in walking distance to the Hospital, as I am – she sounded really welcoming when she phoned & offered me accommodation, last night. She said she has a spare bedroom – I thanked her, it was really kind of her. But I had to tell her that Boris and his wife had also just kindly offered me accommodation, in Toronto, she emailed last night - & I told Anna I had tentatively accepted, though with all the restrictions on travelling etc I wasn't sure how I would get there, to Toronto & their house - I mean with luggage - & I don't know if the buses & trains are still running. (CBC radio news just announced that the PM is very concerned about the nursing-home situation. New rules have been announced. Thank goodness.)

Quite chilly again today! But I must get out for a walk after lunch. So, what do I have for lunch? Cheese & bread & milk!!! Go get it, Jennifer! The fridge almost empty. One way of slimming? Ha ha!

But what else do I have to say here? Maybe my worrying is not so much about the Coronovirus & being shut-in, & the boredom & loneliness & almost-fear (if Angela was still here, maybe we'd find a way of getting together, but they've all long gone home, & the University's shut down – I wonder what they're doing, to keep sane? I thought of emailing her, starting an email correspondence like the one we had before, but I didn't.) The silence & lack of movement are spooky (when did any vehicle last come along this street?). But the garbage was collected this morning – thank goodness I put it out (just in case - remembering that Easter Monday wasn't a local holiday here in the past). Some things don't change!

Tuesday 14th April
KEN

A bright sharp breezy morning! If only this incarceration

could end! But a telephone call from Jimmyboy while I was breakfasting – unusual, he usually emails, but maybe the isolation is getting to him too! (Or he badly wants to keep our emails private!) Anyway, he wants to get together (and so do I, though of course I didn't say so!), but also he seems concerned about Boris's state of health (he has high blood-pressure, & of course, being confined in his wheelchair most of the time, he doesn't get much exercise. And, says James, he seems to be sinking into a deep depression (I know he's vulnerable - Anna mentioned that, when she was his sort-of-companion-housekeeper years ago, he would just go into silence for long periods and she would worry about him, but he had a doctor then who jollied him back into circulation). James said he spoke obsessively, in the telephone conversation, about the Schubert Quintet & that we should all five of us get together, *must* get together, to rehearse it, & even perform it for ourselves! A quaint idea, maybe, but James is taking it seriously. And apparently Boris even talked about us all – Anna, James, Jennifer & me – going to *live* in his house! To rehearse the Quintet, & hopefully a Haydn or Mozart or late-Beethoven quartet or two (like James, I really want to get to know those late-Beethovens).

Come to think of it, maybe it could work – the house is big enough, I remember that - he had me round for dinner was-it-two-years-ago, when my predecessor, I think called Trevor, suddenly got married to an Australian woman & had to be replaced in a hurry – Boris was my viola-teacher. That's when I met James & immediately thought Yes, yes, what a good opportunity!!! – we could be a duet, musically & personally! - & anyway what good fortune it was to find a place for me & my viola in such a successful, well-respected quartet – bloody good luck, & it meant I could continue working downtown (*they* wanted me too!), & maybe eventually buy this condo I'm renting – an ideal arrangement - & it *has* worked out well so far – Yes & a short holiday in Boris's place would be fun, especially if James & I can spend intimate nights together? – So, I said Yes, fine, if we can all manage to do it. Apparently that old housekeeper, can't remember her name, would do all the meals - & of course we would contribute to expenses – Sounds great! Just when we are all getting to the point of going crazy with this unending isolation – enforced now with huge fines, apparently! And soon we'll be legislated into wearing surgical-masks everywhere! Awful! – but could distract attention from my messy too-long hair?

What else? Oh, I was almost forgetting – about James's suggestion that we keep in regular contact by email – he has been keeping a sort of diary, as I guess I have been too (I wonder how many of us, here in what used to be TO's "gay village", have been forced into recording our lives – now they have been emptied of all interesting content!) – but if we retail our thoughts, now that actions are wanting, he says, we can all get to know & understand each other more intimately (not sure I do want that! But why not try it?). He also says we *should* be in intimate contact with each other, we members of an admired Quartet! Even more than we already are. (I think it's all Boris's idea, probably.) It would apparently deepen our sympathetic understanding of each other & "the great music we are privileged to play" (James says Boris said that & I think he really did say that!). Anyway, he is proposing to send us all a sort of introductory message. It will read (James said, & I don't think he was joking): "Dear Fellow Members of the Lark Quartet, I hope you are all keeping well & employing your idleness creatively! As a group of five friends who love music-making, I think we could find mutual cheer & encouragement in directly communicating to each other our thoughts & feelings, & above all playing great music together. Your friend & fellow-musician, James." I think that's more or less correct – but I'll soon be able to check, when his email arrives. Of course, if we do all gather in Boris's house, we'll be in close (too close?) contact anyway. But that intensive emailing could be a good preparation for concord? After all, I hardly know Jenny, the additional Cello, & it will be pleasant to get to know Anna better than has been possible in the few short conversations we've had. Maybe in the end this shut-down will make us better people, more patient & kind (or maybe not!) – as well as reducing pollution around the planet (Eric has sent me an email that features a short film about worldwide reduction of pollution, with liberating effects for wildlife as well as humans, brought to us by the Pandemic – maybe we can *hope* for that, anyway!).

But that reminds me to give a troubled account of news in the media today. First, the horrific state of old-age homes in Quebec & other parts of Canada, no doubt including Ontario, with Seniors suffering not only from COVID-19 but also from being abandoned to filth & death by fleeing Staff (shown as not only being poorly-paid but also terrified of dying themselves – surely governments will *have* to remedy this situation after the Pandemic is finally over? I think Seniors will demand that, the ones who survive). Second, the beginning of political dissension over preparations for, & conduct during, the Pandemic (after the remarkable unity up to now) - especially in the U.S. as the horrific Trump bellows his dishonesty, confusion & incompetence into Brilliant Achievement, or tries to - (surely he won't succeed in bullying & bamboozling his way to a second disastrous Presidency come September?). (There's actually growing concern that he'll declare himself President-for-Life!) And of course there's more, much more, but I'll leave that to posterity to consider, evaluate (of course *this* is not fake-generosity, just fake-news?). Oh, don't try to be clever, Ken. You're out of your depth! So – come, I need a private session with Madame Viola to restore sanity.

FOUR

Wednesday 15th April

ANNA

Gloriously brisk, sunny morning! I'm just back home after a short totter round the block: must keep this old body going! Of course rain is predicted, so the sun will be obscured by heavy clouds pouring in from the West by this afternoon (Spring is still trying to pull away from Winter!), and so one must respond to any opportunity to get some fresh air and exercise. There was no traffic at all; cars were parked all along the street as if it was Sunday, and I saw only one other person, a neighbour taking his dog for a walk (we shouted greetings across the street). Since Hercule died six years ago, I've had no pet – decided it would be too demanding now (dogs should have at least one good walk per day) and also likely more costly than I could afford in retirement (considering the prices that vets charge).

Now I must get on with cleaning the bathroom, and other chores (what will I have for supper? But before that, some light gardening; my daffodils are in flower - I always feel daffs epitomize Spring, in their brilliant yellow; and I'll have my usual short rest after lunch). But I must first record my response when, returned from my walk, I found the latest *Maclean's Magazine* in the mailbox, with some bills etc – bright yellow cover featuring these words: "CORONAVIRUS / HOW DOES THIS END? / A nation in lockdown. A population in peril. We really are in this together." Another harbinger of Spring? But unwelcome, at least to me: there's an air of near-panic around us, and that's negative, destructive. I'll read that "Special Report" later, but surely it can't help Canadians to deal positively with fears and concerns. We must be hopeful, optimistic, determined to make everything better than it was, yes – But here I go, "chattering again, Anna!" as Miss Honikman used to call out, shaming me. All that time ago.

What James has suggested sounds positive and helpful, not only for Boris (if he is descending into another depression), but for the Quintet as a whole, for all of us. James said it was Boris's idea and he was very insistent, so it would be sad to disappoint him – especially as he doesn't seem in a good space, getting very depressed, James said. Boris said there would be no difficulty accommodating us all, and Alice had said she could certainly get in enough food for us all. And it would be so good, so healthy, to be together and playing great music together! "Remember the C Major of this life!" James said.

I'll go on keeping this private diary: it's an old habit, after all, and harmless and also, I think, useful. It'll be easy to email a few words to the four of them each evening, rather than telephoning as I have been, and good to hear from them. So I'll do that, as long as it doesn't evolve into a time-consuming chore!

But let me just summarise the latest "Coronovirus News". Across the world, nearly 2 million COVID-19 infections so far, with about 125,000 deaths (25,000 in USA). There are over 27,000 cases of infection across Canada, 8,000 in Ontario, and a total of almost 1,000 deaths (just yesterday, a reported 75 deaths in Quebec, 43 in Ontario). There is great and growing concern about COVID-19 in Seniors' Nursing Homes, especially in Quebec. Staff are ill or exhausted, so Staffing shortages have become severe, and patients are seriously neglected, and often in isolated and hideously filthy conditions. Horrible! And there are other problems connected with "our nation in lockdown": women virtually imprisoned with their abusers, for instance. Such a distressing litany. Apart from all the reports of financial disaster. Why try to record it all here? But I do. Habit, I guess. It will be a relief, I think, to be in Toronto with the others: no doubt they will also be very troubled, but we'll all be troubled together, which won't be so painful. And we'll be making music!

Oh, a telephone call from Jennifer. She started chattering about this and that, but I could hear the worry, the tension, in her voice. So I told her about my plan, that we, she and I, should accept Boris's invitation – even if James and Ken don't, but I think they will, and anyway they are in Toronto and not far from Boris. I could hear the relief in her voice, and of course she was almost embarrassingly grateful. I said I'd go across in my car to collect her and her luggage in the evening ("Just a small suitcase is all I'll have" she said, so I asked her if she wasn't forgetting something. "Oh, what, my toothpaste?" she replied. "No," I said, "your Cello" and she laughed, "No, I tie it round my neck & drag it wherever I go". I think we'll get on all right, the two of us. I said we'd spend the night here and then drive to Toronto tomorrow morning "And if we're stopped by the RCMP, you'll have to say you're my long-lost little sister" I said). She wondered if it is really all right for us to go to Boris's house and spend a week there with him and Alice, and of course James and Ken too. I said I'm sure that he would have checked that out, if necessary, as it's *his* house and *his* invitation. So that's settled. I'll telephone or send an email to the other four, especially Boris and his wife, to let them know. I also told her I had face-masks, if needed (found in a bathroom drawer: a remnant of my SARS nursing days, obviously).

And now what? Get on, Anna!

Thursday 16th April
JAMES

And what about Pusska, my very dear Pusska, loving companion? "Now that I'm old and feeble, will you discard me? Remember, dear Master, how you saved me from starvation, a painful death? How you lifted me to the warmth and safety of your brave breast, how you took me to your nest and gave me life-preserving milk –" No, I mustn't go on in this sentimental vein. Just to evade the veiled scrutiny of your milky old eyes. We have had eight or is it nine contented years together. Fairly contented. Rarely a sharp human word or sudden feline scratch. And now – But first I'll have to find out how to do it. How to arrange your death, my dear. Because you were a foundling of mature years, I simply assumed that all arrangements relating to your physical state had been made prior to our connection. But now – How could I take you to Boris's, & for all I know he may have acquired a pet, dog or cat, since I was last there – and even then, any pet would probably not have been evident, in his lounge, as I remember he called it, or dining-room. Oh well – maybe I shouldn't go. Of course, if I say I can't, Boris will ask why – & my absence would be a problem for him and the others. I am irreplaceable as First Violin!

Well. I'll pray for inspiration. Maybe one of my neighbours could be persuaded to look after Pusska, or come in to feed him every evening – yes, surely that would work – but oh, I forget Social Distancing etcetera. Actually, on the CBC radio news this morning, & in our local newspaper, intimations of change, even rebellion – people, *some* people, are now questioning the need for social-distancing, for instance. But the bad news continues generally: in yesterday's paper, "Canada's COVID-19 death toll passes 900; economy could shrink 6.2% this year." "27,000 confirmed & presumptive incidents of coronavirus disease" – & in today's paper, over 1,000 of these fatal. On the other hand, Ontario's wildlife is predicted to "experience a population boom" – hear that, Pusska? Maybe, if this or a succeeding Coronavirus takes hold, humans will be wiped off the face of the planet, freeing the rest of "God's Creation" to proliferate & prevail? Stuff for a scifi novel that is surely being written right now! And I should also record that more than half of the Canadian COVID deaths have occurred, often in scandalously horrific circumstances, in long-term-care homes – this should, *must,* force governments to bring about reforms in the health-care of seniors. Jenny will know all about that.

Meanwhile there seems to be growing impatience over the "shut-down of the economy", especially in Trump's USA. And increasing international controversy about how information about the Coronavirus was handled, both by China (accused of deliberately delaying dissemination of information - when it actually began there!) & various Western countries (slowed by bureaucracy, hesitancy, lack of adequate preparation – by democracy itself?).

Oh, what else? I should contact Ken for a chat tonight, about arrangements for transferring ourselves to Boris's place on Saturday (assuming that Anna & Jennifer have both responded positively to his invitation – Anna did, last night & maybe they are already there, at Boris's place, or will be, by the time we arrive. It's not far - we'll go there in my vehicle, I assume (as Ken doesn't have one - I've always been troubled by his reliance on cycling or walking, in Winter especially - carrying his viola on his back! - & of course we'll need some more luggage, for clothes etc – as well as our instruments). I'll also take my laptop, so I can keep in touch with my extensive cohort of friends! They constantly need my affectionate attention!!! And Alice said Boris expected that we'll all have our iphones with us.

So that's IT for now, Pusska. I'd better call Ed about feeding & entertaining you in my absence (good that I stocked up on cat-food several weeks ago, the only variety of it you will deign to eat - because everyone was then talking wildly about Shortages – of toilet-paper especially!).

Friday 17th April
BORIS

Lark News, Volume One, Number One!
From Allegro House, Toronto
Here we go, my dear Colleagues and Lovers of Chamber Music: This is the Newsletter you have been awaiting! In this perilous time, it will provide you with the latest news and views about the Classical Chamber Music we admire and seek to perform at the highest level we can possibly achieve, especially in the present challenging and troubling time when COVID-19 controls our daily lives.

Some of you will remember the series of lunch-hour concerts we have presented at Masterson University over many years – a quarter-century, in fact! During that period the Lark Quartet has changed in its membership, but three of us have been members since the very first concert: the Founder and Cellist, and the First and Second Violins. We're still here!

The Concert that would have celebrated our quarter-century, with our first performance of Schubert's great C-major Quintet (the masterpiece which crowned his short life of glorious creativity), has had to be postponed, like so many artistic endeavors, because of the Covid-19 Crisis; but we hope you will come to our concert on June 15th, which will include quartets by Haydn and Mozart, and celebrate the glory of Summer as well as express our joy and thanksgiving at the end of the Pandemic.

And so on! Alice and I composed this Introduction together. What do you think? If you all agree, we shall share the honour and responsibility of being Guest Editor of this new and exciting journal, which will preserve the memory of our imminent performance of Schubert's noble masterpiece in whose shadow we are assembling, and will also point to a happier future! (As you all probably know, I have long hoped that we would perform the great Quintet! What joy you are giving me!)

Please feel welcome to our humble abode! As you know, I am no longer capable of functioning on Toronto streets and in Toronto stores – this wheel-chair is difficult to move around, even in our home, and without Alice I'm sure I could not survive - I would starve! – so, thank you, dear Alice – you are another of those we honour and thank for your kindness and generosity! Like all doctors and nurses – those evening street-serenades of gratitude that we see and hear on TV are so well deserved!

Writing this, I know that Anna and Jenny will arrive soon and with Alice's help will settle into their room – which I hope is comfortable for you two! I hope you will have a safe journey – I believe even the Queen Elizabeth Way is almost deserted! Alice said the mattresses might be a bit too firm, but when we were sleeping there I thought they were fine - so, as I say, I trust you will be comfortable! James and Ken, you will arrive tomorrow – the two guest-rooms haven't been in use for a few years, so we hope you'll find *your* beds comfortable! Alice has been busy digging out sheets and blankets, she says – from what we used to call "kists" when I was briefly in Cape Town as a boy, after our escape from Nazi Germany just before the War, and before we came to Canada – I can't recall what they're called here, chests? My parents had one in their first store in Toronto, soon after we immigrated, I remember frightening myself by imagining that I had hidden in it and locked myself in - Yes, "kist" - Looking for words, and not finding them, has become a major irritant of my old age!

By the way, I meant to ask this earlier – please don't park behind our vehicle! Alice will need to use it for shopping, which is why it's parked there – but, for your vehicles, there's space for both of them in the Garage – as you'll see when you drive round our car. Sorry to be so – what? Obsessive? Usually I'm only obsessive in the way you know very well – Mind that F#! don't forget that diminuendo! the quaver is important! *Every note counts!* & so on & on!

The news on the CBC this morning was troubling. In Ontario, 564 new cases of the virus, and in Canada as a whole, 30,000 cases now. 170 military personnel are on their way to help in the Quebec long-term-care homes where Staff are ill or have just not returned to work – a dire situation! I hope I've remembered the facts correctly. The situation is obviously serious, though apparently there is hope now that the total number of infections is lessening. Meanwhile, in the US there are cases of right-wing rebellion – people openly defying limitations on being close together, that sort of thing. I know the isolation of young people is becoming less endurable to them, but one hopes they will go on recognizing how important it is, the physical-distancing, for the sake of all of us. (Especially Seniors!)

Enough! You probably know better than I do what is happening! I have been thinking more about Schubert – and especially listening again to that recording I sent all of you, as our starting-point. I'm looking forward so much to having my cello between my knees and playing that glorious music – for too long that's been absent from my life! And I've been thinking – Maybe I should tell you, otherwise you might be hurt or angry with me, that in the last four days I have been informed of the death of a close colleague from my University days, and the death of one of my oldest friends – Death seems to be all around us – but Life will prevail!

So – Onward!

Saturday 18th April
JENNY

Yes, well here we are! Actually it was an easy journey, not many vehicles on the highway, or pedestrians on the pavement, in the City & especially here in Forest Hill. Anna drives carefully – ultra-carefully, actually, & of course she knows her way well, as she once lived in Toronto, & actually in this house!

It's a gloriously sunny breezy day, an English sort of day, I was thinking. And Alice was so welcoming! I liked her immediately, you can tell she is honest & straight-forward - & a hard worker, she obviously had to do a lot of preparation on her own - Boris couldn't help, even if he'd wanted to, & I'm not sure he would have! So she helped us carry our things into the house & up the stairs to this room – which is big & just a little shabby, this would have been the master-bedroom, until he had to have a wheel-chair, & then I suppose he started living in the big dining-room & his study downstairs – I wonder where Alice sleeps, probably on the chesterfield, to be close in case he needs help.

But enough of this – I'm just going to write down important things, won't have time probably to keep a detailed diary like I used to do! Good!

However, continuing bad news on the Covid front. Not a surprise! But disappointing that so many people, mainly young people of course, are so extremely fed up with being housebound that they are starting to go back to their old ways - & that could be disastrous, returning us to "a high incidence of Covid infections", just when they seemed to be levelling-off. What will our authorities do to restore control, without losing public respect? And, talking of public respect, the second problem is of course the suffering & deaths of elderly men & women in Long-term-care Homes – agonizing for families & friends, who have found their loved-ones suffering in filth & despair. It's a huge problem of neglect, over many years, that will require a lot of work & money & political will to remedy. Family-members are clearly upset & angry. So, major problems - & at a time when, after Covid is brought under control, public finance will be so diminished by all the financial help that the Federal & Provincial Governments have been increasingly providing.

And the Covid figures announced today (I heard this on the CBC News, while Anna was driving us along the QEW, which was very quiet) – well, I hope I'm remembering this accurately – Over 500 deaths, 85 new cases today, & 10,000 cases altogether in Ontario (can that really be right?). Then there was a whole programme about the treatment (mistreatment?) of Seniors in the long-term-care systems, all of them under the control of

Provincial Governments – health-care workers are demanding those governments urgently take control of all long-term-care homes, & reform the whole system – but will that happen? Anna didn't think it so, she was very skeptical, she said it all made her angry and she told me some of her experiences as a young trainee-nurse during the SARS Epidemic – even the doctors (*especially* the doctors, she said) refused to wash their hands! Said they didn't have time!

Well, that's enough. I must go to bed. Anna is still with Boris, I think they're planning rehearsals, probably also talking about the past! The mattress looks a bit lumpy but it's probably all right – I'm so sleepy, anyway. I think we were all a bit constrained at Supper, that's what Alice called it, and James & Ken were tense & didn't say much – they had arrived a few hours after us, & I think they're not too happy about being in separate rooms – that's if they're gay lovers, as I guess they are, but I may be wrong. I'm not an expert! But they live quite near each other in what they called 'the gay village' – which, they were saying, had changed a lot & I must visit it when that becomes possible! And all the time I was thinking 'But I won't be in the Quartet then!' of course - & if Boris doesn't think I'm good enough, when we rehearse the Schubert Quintet, I won't be in the Quintet either! But at least they have to put up with me here & now! And it will be an interesting experience, Jennifer! So to bed, to bed, & tomorrow to fresh fields.

Sunday 19th April
KEN

I slept in! Which implies that the bed is quite comfortable. I wonder if James slept well? Of course he's a good twenty or so years older than me (I think – should ask him) & he's not in good condition – told me he doesn't work out, just relies on walking. Now we're separated for the week (he says Boris definitely wants us all to stay here till next Sunday evening – which is beginning to seem like a long time - & already I'm wondering how Pusska is, in his new quarters – which I hope he won't decide is his new home!). I've been thinking that it may be time to have a real talk with James – here there should be time for that, neither of us can run away (I admit I have mostly been the guilty one!), & Boris & Schubert are a perfect combo, I think, to keep us calm & focused. Worth a try, for both of us & maybe the rest of the Quartet too. Anyway, I should go down & join the others & see what's happening, if anything! The water wasn't very hot, so I decided not to shower (I'll ask that woman, Alice, is that her name, she seems to run the house, if it can be hotter?). James always has a cold shower, even in winter (brr!) – but I need the heat! I managed to shave & at least make myself look clean. I hope. So now –

I did listen to the CBC as I woke up, the News, on the bedside radio – can't recall the new COVID numbers, but they were bad, especially the number of deaths in old-age homes - & apparently there's an increasing feeling now (especially, I'd assume, among the young) that self-isolation & physical-distancing aren't really necessary any more – but the authorities say it's too early, & dangerous, to "return to normal" – so we'll see what happens. "Non-essential travel" is what we're told to avoid - I told Boris I had wondered if travelling here could be considered "essential" & he said "Of course". Then I asked him if joining his household, the four of us, could be considered legitimate – he shrugged & smiled & said "You're here. What's the problem? Don't you feel welcome? You're a member of the Lark family. Oh what Larks!" When we arrived, I looked to see if there was any sign that anyone in the other mansions, admittedly far apart, along the street, might be watching – no sign of that, no movement, so I guess he was right. Apparently, too, stunt-driving & street-racing is happening now, along empty streets. But I wonder if we were just fortunate yesterday, driving across to here, not to be stopped & questioned by police? Were we disobeying any actual regulation? I hope not – just left that to James to decide, as he was driver & it's his vehicle. Guess COVID-19 doesn't need our help to prevail.

STOP this, Ken! No sound of movement, but GET DOWN-STAIRS & see if "Breakfast is Served"! If Jimmyboy has beaten me to it, he'll smile that superior smile (I wonder if he knows it infuriates me?). Maybe it's a good thing that we're separated - though it didn't seem that at first, especially with Anna & Jenny being together. (Suddenly occurred to me – does James wonder if, because of my disappearing act, I may have contracted the Virus? Surely not. But if so, surely he'd be glad we're in separate rooms?)

I guess I must look like a servant. That woman who presided over breakfast asked me if she could dictate the second LARK NEWS to me – is she Boris's wife, or secretary? Apparently she has "problems with the computer" (don't we all?) – Boris has told her to do that, & then through the rest of the week, each member of the Quintet will be required to contribute one of the daily items. What a bully he is – BAAS BORIS!!!! Another Trump. But maybe only that type of man could create & control a Quartet! So we allow him to scan our most intimate thoughts & news – why? Maybe because we assume he doesn't have the patience to be concerned about anything other than his personal ambitions & interests & concerns. And music. (Am I being sarcastic again? James accuses me of that. "Musicians are such egotists" he says – "Except me. I'm exceptional.") Anyway, I'll go find Alice now & she can deliver wisdom for me to send forth (separately from this diary-entry of course!) (Am I beginning to talk to myself? Or am I merely very tense in this wealthy-but-shabby house?) Madam, your obsequious secretary is ready. Dictate away!

LARK NEWS & VIEWS, Volume One, Number Two
I think you all know that Schubert's String Quintet in C Major was composed near the end of his life. After it, he composed only the three final Piano Sonatas and (of course!) some songs. He was born in 1797 and died in 1828, aged only thirty-one. He had lived all his life in Vienna, mostly in poverty. By the time he composed the Quintet, he had composed six symphonies (I have always loved the "Unfinished Symphony"!), an almost countless number of glorious songs, and many admired chamber-works. You know all this. (Boris says I married him because of our mutual love of Schubert, and I say No, just for himself, that's more than enough, and he always replied "No, because of that Quintet, and we'll perform

it one day, before I die!" So now we are all here, the Quartet he started half a century ago, and the plan is for rehearsing and performing a movement every day of this week, and then put them together for a complete performance next Saturday!

Of course, when we planned a performance of Schubert's Quintet, we didn't know that COVID-19 would be so very destructive, that so many people would lose jobs and income, and that most stores and facilities would be closed – and, as you know, we had to cancel all the Lark concerts we had planned and even advertised. You know all this, but Boris said "We mustn't give in, we must stand firm" and I know you agree, love and music conquer all. So here we are, and welcome to our home! As Boris says, "Music will always prevail", I'm sure you've heard him say that. Thank you!

FIVE

What? When? Where? Who? Why?

And what is our failure here but a triumph's evidence
For the fullness of the days? Have we withered or agonized?
Why else was the pause prolonged but that singing might issue
    thence?
Why rushed the discords in but that harmony should be prized?
Sorrow is hard to bear, and doubt is slow to clear,
Each sufferer says his say, his scheme of the weal and woe:
But God has a few of us whom he whispers in the ear;
The rest may reason and welcome: 'tis we musicians know.

(From "Abt Vogler", by Robert Browning – Boris's favourite poem; he declaimed passages from it soon after I met him, and then often later to me and anyone nearby; he seemed to know it by heart - a very long poem – I used to joke that it represented all he knew of English Literature, including Shakespeare!)

And now, as penance for my somehow losing the email record of all the Quartet messages during the week when we rehearsed the Quintet for our Concert on Saturday 25th April, I shall draw on my defective memory to compensate for that loss. This will be my apology and tribute to Boris. All I can offer now! Here goes:

(Oh, first one comment about the circumstances. As we all know, our country, like most countries, is afflicted by the coronavirus COVID-19; and this mysterious disease, for which there is currently no cure, dominates our lives. Unless a cure is miraculously found, that situation may continue for an unpredictable period, maybe many years. So we must get used to it! But there is surely no need to despair! I am not clever enough to offer wisdom – but I will say that Music and Poetry offer relief and inspiration. Our Concert was surely inspired! Our Quartet – Boris's Quartet - may not survive, but its legacy does, in our memories and music-making! The Pestilence of COVID-19 also continues, but surely it will not prevail, if we are determined and positive in our response to it. We must stop destroying the planet on which we live, we must work hard and constantly to prevent violence and warfare, we must create art, we must enjoy our brief lives and make life enjoyable for all humans and animals. We should, we must! That's what I think. And then we will hear it – "the C Major of this life".)

FINAL COMMENTS on Schubert's QUINTET in C Major
(Recalling as much and as accurately what the five of us – Boris, James, Ken, Jennifer and I, Anna –wrote for Boris in the diary-entries he ordained.)

Schubert composed his Quintet in C Major during the summer of 1828. In a letter written on October 2nd that year, he referred to an imminent private rehearsal of the Quintet; but he was very ill by then, and died on November 19th 1828. So he probably never heard his Quintet, and it wasn't performed until 1850.

1. For the Comments written when we were rehearsing the Quintet, before our performance on Saturday 25th April 2020, the First Movement (*Allegro ma non troppo*) was allocated to James - a good choice as, being First Violin, he had to set pace and intensity. I remember Boris telling him, during our rehearsing that Monday, "Go for it! Let's go for it! Schubert wants us to take notice, that's why the First Movement is so forceful and abrupt, and you notice that the melody is in C Minor – just the first of many unusual keys and unexpected key-shifts – Schubert is famous for them." Later in the movement, the two cellos (Boris and Jennifer) play a sort of duet – in the key of Eb, one of the many unexpected key-shifts in this Movement, and also in the Quintet as a whole. The movement, as a whole, is exhilarating, I think, and there are glorious passages when the two cellos sing together, and the viola and cello have a conversation!

I remember James saying afterwards that he had not known how fine that Movement is – like me, he had always considered it as primarily an introduction to the marvellous Second Movement! James also commented, if I remember rightly, on the cello duet that Boris and Jennifer had played so beautifully – I could see that he was impressed by her confident reading of the score, and the way she partnered Boris so accurately (of course there were some lapses, for Boris to stop and require repeats, but he was generally satisfied – indeed, my impression was that he generally admired her playing). And the rest of us did our bit, of course.

2. Tuesday: Jennifer commented on the Second Movement (*Adagio*): I felt almost jealous that Boris had given that to her! How I have loved loved LOVED this glorious Slow Movement since I first heard it many years ago, as a girl of (I think) sixteen! And I have listened to it again (as performed on the CD recording that Boris gave each one of us) countless times. This is music so ethereal, so – well, I run out of superlatives; it is such a joy and privilege to hear it! To participate in creating it!

The movement, in E Major, is dominated by a long, flowing violin melody, an ecstatic dialogue between cellos and violin, with a *pizzicato* bass; and then there is a loud, restless middle section; before it finally returns to the serene E major theme. Of course, there's much more to it – but, really, one must listen and listen to it, and marvel at its calm endless beauty – or rather, one longs for it to be endless! But life, and the Quintet, must continue.

After the performance of this movement, Jennifer sat in quiet stillness for some minutes, but I noticed that Boris was in tears.

3. Wednesday: Third Movement (*Scherzo: Presto* and *Trio: Andante sostenuto*). Ken's comments. He wrote only a short commentary.

"Imperious, demonic" he said. "I remember a critic writing that about this Scherzo. I think of it as cheerful, uninhibited music – a strong contrast with the preceding movement – *and* with the *Trio,* which, in the totally unexpected key of D♭, is surprisingly gloomy, almost despairing. When the scherzo returns, it resumes the boisterous, enigmatic uncertainty of its first appearance."

4. The final Movement, *Allegretto*. Thursday: I remember Ken calling this Movement an "idealized Viennese dance"! Well, it is certainly a fine contrast to the Scherzo, but, as Ken said, it does not, cannot, clear away the sad grey clouds that have threatened to end all cheerfulness throughout the Movement.

I'm not suggesting (and I don't think Ken did) that the entire Quintet is sorrowful – no, it's not, but sorrow lurks and often intrudes, even though vigorous delight finally wins. Or – not quite! Yes, there is joy in this, the Quintet's concluding movement. BUT the joy is threatened by gloom – in other words, there is a full representation of both extremes, sorrow as well as happiness, in this glorious music, as it ends. Happiness wins, I think – but only just!

The final chord *is* C Major, but it is almost contradicted, Boris said, by a penultimate "Neapolitan second" that momentarily holds off the final, satisfying tonic chord. "Schubert questions his own optimistic C Major," Boris said, "even as he is concluding his greatest creation; for, as he knows, as we all know, life is not endlessly happy: it includes suffering, and it comes to an end". (Yes, like the suffering brought by COVID-19, but Schubert and Boris say that joy will return – will win in the end!)

SIX

Sunday 26th April
ANNA

Disaster! I am trying to face my dreadful failure, before telling the others. So soon after Boris left us. They will be devastated, as I am devastated.

The performance of Schubert's Quintet – No audience, except for dear Alice, but it was glorious, unforgettable, it will always be unforgettable. And there we sat, next morning, in Boris's home, relaxed, weary and happy. The concert had been a moving tribute – oh, to Boris certainly, and the Quartet that he had founded and led for a quarter-century; and of course to Schubert and his great composition (which we had performed with precision and delight); and to the divine gift, the great joy, of music; and to the Creator (Robert Browning would add) who gave us that gift, to help us endure the anxious sadness inflicted by the Pandemic and the dreadful murders in Nova Scotia. Yes. That can never be taken from us, none of it; our intense emotions, our deep memories. But –

Maybe we sensed that all was not well. We were all there, sitting around the table – James, Ken, Jennifer and myself – eating cornflakes and toast, chatting desultorily. Weary but content, as I say.

But where was Boris? We had been expecting to hear his wheelchair approaching. Preceded by his loud voice. But - Silence.

Then Alice came quietly into the room and stood near the door, just stayed there, with tears running down her cheeks. James stood up, went round the table to her, and took her hand. I think we knew then, I think we already knew, that Boris was dead.

After a moment, Alice said hesitantly "It was what he wanted. He asked me to thank you all for coming, and for performing the Quintet with him, and to say this to you, 'My resting-place is found, / The C Major of this life: so, now I will try to sleep.' I hope I've remembered that right."

"Yes," James said quietly, "you have. Thank you." He put his arm around her, and they stood together.

And I hope *I* got it right, too. My memory is poor now, and getting worse all the time. But I think we were all still puzzled. Obviously his death had not been sudden, unexpected.

"It's what he wanted" Alice repeated. "He planned it, and asked me not to tell anyone. You know Canadian law allows that now, 'medically-assisted suicide' I think they call it, and he had cancer as well as heart-disease. His doctor came early this morning, as Boris had requested. Only she and I were there with him - when he passed - and she has made all arrangements. He told me he didn't want a burial service, or a memorial service. 'The Schubert Quintet was my memorial service.' That's what he said.

"He had made all the arrangements, with the doctor, for – his 'departure' is what he called it - and for his body to be cremated. He made me promise not to tell anyone beforehand, he didn't want any 'fuss', he said. I was unwilling, he could see that. But after a while, I agreed. I had to. He was so determined. He wouldn't rest until I agreed, and I could see of course that my reluctance was upsetting him even more, and causing him even more pain.' She drew a deep tremulous breath. 'His doctor came, she was with us. And they will come to take his body soon. So if you wish to say farewell, you should go in now.'

After a few moments, we went slowly into his bedroom, and stood silently near him for a while. I think I was still almost paralysed by the shock, and struggling to focus my mind. I could only think "The C Major of this life" and "My resting-place is found." He certainly looked more composed than I would have expected – more relaxed, almost smiling, lying there on his back, with the blanket pulled up to his chin.

Jennifer took my hand as we left the room, and held it tight. James and Ken went ahead of us. Alice was already clearing away the remains of our breakfast.

After a few moments of uncertainty, Jennifer and I went out into the garden. The two men followed, and the four of us sat in tense silence at the picnic-table until Ken said, loudly, almost angrily, "Well, I'm going for a walk", and set off. James, after a moment of hesitation, followed him. Jennifer and I went back into the house to help Alice in the kitchen.

But I haven't told you about my subsequent sad discovery. Whatever the cause (I have to think it was almost certainly my ineptitude), a long segment of my computer record of the period (Monday 20th to Thursday 23rd of April) leading up to our performances (Friday 24th and Saturday 25th of April) disappeared. Did I delete it by mistake? Surely not! But I must have, otherwise how could it happen? Four days gone – just gone, utterly *gone!* Just as we will all be gone soon. - And commentaries on each day by James, Ken, Jennifer and myself. Our complete daily diary record, such as it was. I told Jennifer about this catastrophe, and she tried to recover what was lost; she knows much more than I do about computers; but it was indeed 'lost and gone forever'. Fortunately, the diary-entries (by me) for our final two days here (after the Performances on Friday and Saturday) have survived. Of course the others probably have a record of their comments on the Quintet rehearsals, and our performance, but Jennifer said it would be a lot of trouble for them, and probably distressing, to read their comments again now; and anyway, did it matter, we all had to move on.

Jennifer could see how upset I was. She tried to comfort me, and when I said "What will I tell the others?" she said "Nothing. They won't ask. We're all having to deal with Boris's death and with our plans for the immediate future. Soon we'll be leaving, all except Alice, we should talk to her about her situation. And we all have to face issues about *our* future."

"Will you come and live with me?" I asked, to my own surprise.

"Oh, Anna. Thank you. Let's talk about that. You've been so good to me."

So I was left in continuing uncertainty. But I could see that she was mulling over the idea.

"It's about Ken" she said suddenly.

"Yes, I know."

"You *know*? Did he say anything to you? Surely he wouldn't – and he has to think about James, you must know they have been close for some time?"

"James knows too. Jennifer, we should talk, all four of us, while we're together here. If we all agree. I think James is upset and hurt, they've been together for at least two years – more or less, though James told me they're having some difficulties in their relationship. So he was very quick to notice that Ken was attracted to you, wanted to be with you, talk to you – he even spoke to me a bit about that. And when you went for those late-afternoon walks with Ken last week, after the Quintet rehearsals –"

"Keeping a couple of yards apart – ! Not very obviously romantic, but maybe, when we are all so tense because of the CO-VID-19 situation – So many changes are coming, once this crisis is over - so many changes are already happening – we can see already that our lives will be very different – So. I think Ken and I were really just exploring our impressions of each other. I like him, I really like him, he's lively, he's fun – but I like him as a friend, and that's what I decided I'm going to tell him."

Well, I've tried to recall that conversation as accurately as I can. It clarified our relationship, Jennifer's and mine. She also told me, I forgot to say this, that Ken said James hoped, if the Quartet continues, maybe under another name, that she would take Boris's place as cellist. Really, it doesn't seem right to be thinking and talking about such things, so soon after Boris's death; but maybe we have all been thinking of the future, we must all have seen how old he was, and frail - even though we didn't know how sick he actually was.

This is what I wrote sometime earlier, on a loose page that I've just found:

When we started the week of rehearsing the Quintet, Boris asked me to take over from him as "Editor" of our diary-pieces – he said he'd been too busy with the rehearsals, and anyway hadn't had much time (or, I now think, desire) to read what we had been writing (at his request, of course!). He sounded as if he regretted, or half-regretted, the whole thing – but it was *his* idea, after all! (He told me at the beginning that it was a way for each of us to get to know the other Quintet members as well as possible. But in fact it was not a good way, or very practicable.) Now, I think he may have been exhausted as well as ill – much worse, physically and emotionally, than we realized; and maybe not thinking things out very clearly. Anyway, I agreed. Though when the whole record of that week, together with our thoughts about the four movements of the Quintet, suddenly disappeared on my laptop computer, I felt both guilty and very stupid. And I didn't dare tell him: it would have been just before the great Quintet performance! (It was like the occasion when I somehow lost a diamond ring inherited from my maternal grandmother - and never told my mother! And was always fearful that she would ask me why I never wore it!)

Friday 24th April
ANNA

What a glorious day! Sun shining cheerfully, breeze ruffling the daffodils in the garden; magnolias in flower, cherry-trees in blossom; lovely, lovely! After breakfast, we sat for a while – all of us – on the deck. In silence. Then Boris cleared his throat and announced the day's agenda (no consultation, of course!). The morning is ours! We are permitted to walk and talk! Alice will go to the Supermarket to stock up on vegs and fruit, for lunch today and for tomorrow. In the afternoon, we will play two favourite quartets which we have performed quite recently (of course he has all the parts here) – Haydn's "Emperor", No. 62, in C Major (which we have played often over the years, a great favourite! I think Boris identifies with the Emperor! The second movement, I remember, is a set of variations on the famous theme that became a national anthem and a hymn-tune, I think); and then Mozart's "Dissonance" quartet, KV 465, in C Major. Neither of them is challenging for us, and James was clearly disappointed that we won't be playing one of Beethoven's Last Quartets, as he had hoped – but he said nothing, probably recognizing that it wouldn't be possible to play one of those without considerable rehearsal. I thought that once again Boris's aversion to Beethoven was in play, and I wondered again about the cause – it's always been an issue with him (clearly James would agree with me, though he and I have never discussed this), and I think it has weakened our Quartet's reputation - occasionally a critic, here or abroad, has noticed the lack of Beethoven in our programmes and commented on that. Anyway, too late to debate it, and I know Boris would just swat any criticism away: he has always been Boss! And after all, he did found the Quartet.

Sunday 26th April

The news, on the radio, is ever more distressing and disturbing. Further information has emerged about the Nova Scotia murders that has stunned this nation and provoked a cry of horror and sadness. Almost unbelievably, 22 people were murdered, not far from Truro (I was born and grew up near there, so I know the area well, although I haven't been back there for many years). The perpetrator was wearing an RCMP uniform and drove a vehicle made to look just like an RCMP cruiser, and the whole rampage seems to have been sparked by an argument between the gunman and his girlfriend (who managed to escape him and give crucial information to the police – but she too, like the relatives and friends of all the victims, will be tormented, I think, by memories of the slaughter for the rest of her life). All that happened, I think, just after, or maybe even during, our performance of the Schubert Quintet. Hearing more details about it this morning on the radio was of course very distressing. As a Maritimer, maybe I was more intensely affected than the others.

We watched and listened to the CBC TV News that evening in silence. Boris and Alice weren't there – he was no doubt exhausted, after our rehearsals and especially our performance of the Quintet, and maybe he was also in great pain. None of us commented then on the murders in Nova Scotia. I guess we were too exhausted, after our concert, and all the rehearsing before it. And what was there to say? What happened was beyond words. Sheer horror. I hardly dare to think about it still. It was, and is, the very opposite of our performance of Schubert's glorious music.

And then there is also the continuing account of the COVID-19 Corona Virus spreading and killing around the world. Here, in Canada, a total so far of about 45,000 cases, with 2,500 deaths; in Ontario alone, over 13,500 cases, 750 deaths. There's increasing tension over the 'lock-downs', though not (yet?) here as angry as in the US. And much discussion and concern about the likely long-term effects of the disease itself, on national economies and the lives of populations in so many countries around the world.

So we are now surrounded by sorrow and worry. Sometimes I wondered - and maybe the others did too, Should our performance go ahead? And that was *before* the murders in Nova Scotia – which, as I said, we learned about after our concert. Clearly Boris wanted us to go ahead – performing the Quintet was maybe, for him, the Last Rite?

After breakfast that morning (Saturday 25th April), Alice pushed him in his wheelchair out onto the deck, and we followed dutifully. It was cool but sunny, a glorious Spring morning. When we were all seated, Boris cleared his throat, indicating that he had something important to say. "I know we are all troubled by the news of suffering, in Canada and around the world. But we also know that there is triumphant good in our world. I am remembering one of the great poems about the endless conflict between good and evil. It is also a poem about the ultimate triumph of goodness over evil. And it is about the power of music. Yes, you will remember it, I have quoted it before, often, often - Robert Browning's 'Abt Vogler'. Let me recite some of the lines I have known so well for most of my life. 'There shall never be one lost good! What was, shall live as before; / The evil is null, is nought, is silence implying sound; / What was good shall be good ... / On the earth the broken arcs; in the heaven, a perfect round.' Also 'Sorrow is hard to bear, and doubt is slow to clear, / Each sufferer says his say, his scheme of the weal and woe; / But God has a few of us whom he whispers in the ear; / The rest may reason and welcome: 'tis we musicians know.' Yes, Schubert, our beloved Musician, *he* knew. And yes, we musicians *do* know. And the poem ends, you may recall these words, I have often quoted them: "… I have dared and done, for my resting-place is found, / The C Major of this life: so, now I will try to sleep." The Abbot Vogler's instrument was of course a church organ, but I think his thoughts and words apply very directly to us. Yes, we musicians know - When I read Browning's poem for the first time, I was a boy still struggling to deal with memories of the Holocaust – which destroyed all my relatives, apart from my parents. I was - But now, let us prepare for our concert, for the joy and privilege of performing, on our five instruments, what for me is one of the greatest works of music ever composed. We have rehearsed each movement, now we are ready to perform the whole Quintet. You have the rest of the morning to relax. Then, this afternoon –'the C Major of this life'", and he gestured to Alice, who carefully pushed him indoors.

I should say that my rendition of Boris's speech is obviously unlikely to be totally accurate. However, I have heard him make that speech before, in its essentials – one essential being those passages from a poem he has long admired (I remember his recommending it to me soon after I met him, and that I read it then, for the first time, as a young woman - in about 1970, I think).

James, who would have been similarly imbued with the poem (he has known Boris almost as long as I have), smiled at me, then sat down beside me. Quietly he said "Yes, the C Major of this life. You noticed that the two quartets we performed yesterday -"

"- are in C Major. Yes, I did notice, one could hardly miss it. Of course it wasvery deliberate, surely?"

"Yes. Surely. But exactly what does that mean?"

Of course all this was not only before the Quintet concert but before we knew about the Nova Scotia massacre, which also makes me think of "Abt Vogler" – "The evil is null, is nought, is silence implying sound; / What was good shall be good, with, for evil, so much good more …" (But is it, is it?)

And so, our performance. Really, it was extremely demanding to perform that programme – even if to no audience other than ourselves and Alice (who stood beside Boris and turned the pages for him). But we were inspired. I don't think we ever performed the Haydn and Mozart quartets better, on the Friday afternoon (24th April); and then Schubert's Quintet flowed gloriously the next afternoon (25th April). Were there errors, deficiencies, in our performance? Oh yes, yes - "But God has a few of us whom he whispers in the ear; / The rest may reason and welcome; 'tis we musicians know." And I think we all *did* know. Afterwards, after the beautiful melodies, after those final questing chords, when the last echoes died away, we sat for how many minutes, maybe ten minutes, exhausted.

Then, a loud clapping. By Boris. Who was also weeping, sobbing. Alice helped him from his chair to his wheelchair, and pushed him in silence from the room. And the rest of us sat on for a while, in silence.

And the next morning (Sunday 19th April), news of the murders in Nova Scotia. But, while we were sitting there with our brunch of coffees and toast, a further shock was about to strike us. James had just turned off the radio. "Do we want to hear any more? Horrible!" "I wonder where Boris and Alice are" I said. "Probably still asleep, exhausted" James said. And maybe I was thinking "He's an old man, after all, and sick – was it all too demanding for him?"

Then Alice came into the room slowly. She said "Boris" and began to weep. "Here, sit down, Alice" James said, and helped her to a chair. "What's happened, are you all right, is Boris all right?" And she whispered "He's dead."

After sipping some coffee that I put in front of her, she began a hesitant explanation. I had assumed – knowing his health had been weakening – that he might have suffered a heart-attack during the night. But that was wrong. As Alice explained eventually, his death had been organized for some months, with the acceptance of his doctor (who arrived within the hour, accompanied by a nurse, and who dismissed us while she organized the removal of Boris's body). James asked tentatively about saying Farewell, and Alice, leaning on him, went with him into the bedroom. The rest of us followed slowly.

Then we went outside into the garden – Jennifer, Ken and myself - and sat there in silence. When James joined us, he said quietly to me that we should look after Alice. But Alice didn't need looking after by then. She told us that Boris had planned his death months before. Because he had not only a weak heart but cancer in its late stages, and could not live much longer, his wish had been officially approved, under the new legislation.

"I don't really understand why he was so secretive" James said. "And now I can see that he was actually challenging us to guess what he was up to. 'The C Major of this life' – two quartets in C Major, and, above all, our performance of Schubert's Quintet, a work that he said he'd loved and admired throughout his life, and had longed to perform, and now, finally - All of this adding up to an announcement of his intention. I hope he has found joy on the other side."

(Have I repeated myself? I think so. And there's probably some confusion in this account, especially around Boris's death and its aftermath. I apologise to anyone reading this text for any confusion (which is an indication of incipient Alzheimer's, no doubt – as well as grief). My life is changing, our lives are changing.)

And that's IT. Finished? A story of our lives – or, rather, a few recent fragments of our broken and uncertain lives. No different, fundamentally, from other lives. And of course from all human life, all life on this planet, threatened now by COVID-19. What will happen? The latest Canadian COVID-19 numbers are 50,000 cases, 3,000 deaths - and the Government's financial deficit to this point is $250 billion. How long will it take for Canada and Canadians to recover, when COVID-19 ends? Will we ever recover? And meanwhile, what of this polluted planet?

(When did I write that?)

Friday 8th May

My final entry! I'll be glad to dispense with this "diary": it was Boris's idea, after all: an attempt, as far as he explained it, to make us all close friends, so as to achieve the best possible performances of the chamber-music he so admired; and ultimately of Schubert's Quintet. A noble Farewell. Did it work? I don't think so - if one notes the tension that increased among us, especially between James and Ken, but even between Boris himself and the rest of us. (I think he realized that, eventually.) Too much information! But maybe it also underlay the intense daily 'rehearsals' of each of the Quintet's four movements in that final week before our 'concert' (an audience of one, if you exclude the players: just dear Alice, whom I shall miss so much; more about that later!); but maybe, ironically, it also helped us all to become, again, miraculously, a unified musical 'machine': bad word; but what word could convey the living power of the music, together with our necessary collusion, our loving respectful determination to honour Boris, our Quartet, and above all, Schubert? Enough of that. " ... here is the finger of God .../ Existent behind all laws, that made them and, lo, they are!" Yes, enough, Anna! As Boris would have said to me – as he did once, actually, in one of his frequent critical comments during our early years, "You are so stupid, Anna!"

So, Jennifer and I will leave here after lunch, which Alice is preparing as I write. I suggested that she come with us to Hamilton, for a break – but of course that isn't really possible in present circumstances, as she immediately pointed out. "We will keep in touch by telephone" she said. Yes, Alice, I think we will, and she and I will be able to live together into our old age, if we both want that. I will talk to Jennifer about the situation. She told me, when we started getting ready to leave, yesterday, that James had hinted she might take Boris's place as cellist, "if our Quartet continues" (but how can it, when Boris was not only the Founder but our absolute leader?). She is clearly restless, as I was at her age, when I was in thrall to Boris. And then there's her relationship, whatever it is or was, with Ken. Maybe, when the COVID-19 Plague is over, if it ever is, she will give up her Gerontology studies at university and decide to live in Toronto

- as she once said she'd like to do? Or go West, where, I think she said, she has some relatives. So many uncertainties! And so many opportunities, at her age – or there should be.

Above all, there's the huge continuing problem of COVID-19! Just recently, with the Schubert performance, and Boris's death, I have almost forgotten about that! Yet it continues, and maybe intensifies; and even as more and more communities in Canada and especially the United States (far from united about this!) are "opening up", whole populations are struggling impatiently to maintain rules about social separation and so on – and increasingly there is resistance and impatience, while Governments and their health authorities try to maintain appropriate, safe behaviour. How long can that situation go on? I fear that it will all end in disaster; but that may be the pessimism and weariness of old age!

It's now Friday 8th of May, and I will end here. Nothing much more to record. I never kept a diary earlier in my life, and have no wish to continue writing this. (Who would ever read it anyway? Would I?) Today, I learned from CBC Radio news as I awoke, is the 75th anniversary of D Day, the day that the Second World War ended in Europe. We should never, never forget that! Of course the atom-bombing of Hiroshima and Nagasaki was still to come, and *they* should never be forgotten either – and only then would that War be fully over. But still, it was the beginning of a new beginning, D Day, a New Dawn! Wasn't it? No, don't answer.

Anyway, I'll end with the latest COVID-19 information, incomplete as it may be. I imagine many in Canada try to follow, and remember, the latest facts and figures. Why? Well, we all need a general understanding of how we should behave, for the good of all, in the present conditions of our daily lives! (Though there may be surprises, even for Jennifer and me as we return to Hamilton this afternoon.) Anyway, here is the present state of the Coronovirus Plague. Yesterday, Thursday 7th May: Globally, over 250,000 COVID-19 deaths. Across Canada, over 60,000 cases of COVID-19 reported, and Canada's coronavirus death toll has passed 5,000, I think, more than 1,000 of those in long-term care institutions. In Ontario, 1,361 deaths in all. (Toronto alone, by the end of April, had recorded 5,550 cases, with 365 deaths – "shocking numbers" some medical authority commented.) But also "60-70% of Canadians support a slow easing of measures to control the spread of COVID-19". Notably more masks are being worn along the streets, apparently, and "social separation" (keeping 6 feet apart from other humans, in public places) is being generally maintained. More than 3 million Canadians have lost their jobs owing to COVID-19, and the total number of those now out-of-work is well over 5 million. Yes, a disaster, a disaster.

So what is our future? On this cool Spring day (Friday 8th May 2020), I look out at the garden: daffodils still in bloom, swaying bright yellow in the breeze; magnolias and cherry-trees in glorious pink blossom. "Joyous Spring" says Nature, poor wounded Nature. And our response? Do we have one?

Tuesday 12 May
(I think) (A glorious sunny day!)

James and Ken departed before Jennifer and I did. They were obviously stiff and cool with each other (and with Jennifer and me), but hopefully they would have relaxed during their short journey. James was very affectionate towards Alice, insisting on a 'get-together ASAP'. When I enquired (tactfully, I hope) about her longer-term future plans, Alice said she was 'thinking of turning the house into a residence for students and a few elderly women'; but hoped to accept my invitation to visit me in Hamilton as soon as possible. And then she suddenly started talking about Boris again. I was surprised, and just listened, mostly in silence. Not that I couldn't understand her emotions, thinking too that she will now be on her own, at least until the Pandemic lessens, and with nobody to talk to – well, nobody who would immediately understand. But also some of what she said was new to me. In our years together, Boris did not talk much about his past, for whatever reason – well, I do think he was inclined to look down on me as an immature female! He was a man of his generation; he didn't take women, especially young women, seriously.

Anyway, to summarise some of what she said. Recently, before the invitation to us for the Quintet concert, when he 'became obsessed with that', she said, Boris had talked more and more about his youthful years in Cape Town; he had enjoyed the warm climate, the sea-swimming and mountain-climbing, as any young boy would – especially after the constriction and fear of being Jewish in Hitler's Germany. But his Father had decided, when the War ended, to emigrate to Canada; he had learnt that some cousins who had survived the Holocaust were settled and prospering in Toronto, and he was also disturbed by what became known to us all in later years as Apartheid; in Cape Town there was a vigorous population of "Cape Coloureds", people of mixed race who lived in a crowded area called "District Six" – I don't know why I remember that when I can remember hardly any other names!

Boris told her that he had loved the free-and-easy lifestyle, and had friends who taught him to enjoy music and dancing – did you know he was a great dancer in his youth? (No, Alice, I would never have guessed that!) In Canada, he was sent to a prominent boarding-school where he was beaten and abused: his Father had quickly become quite wealthy, as a partner in a prominent company established by relatives. Boris became rebellious, refused to join the company, and "travelled the world", he said, as a young man. Then he returned to Toronto, after his Father died unexpectedly, leaving him this house as well as, he said, "a small fortune"; so he was able to study and teach music for the rest of his life. "It's all I ever wanted" he told Alice. "Learning, teaching, enjoying the greatest music ever composed." Well, I wondered. But then, he had never given me what I knew he could have given – encouragement, gratitude. He had eventually been appointed to a research position at the University, and, Alice said, he became fascinated by Medieval literature, and at that time read and reread Boccaccio's *Decameron,* on which he had become a "recognized expert", giving lectures on it occasionally. About a group of young aristocratic Italians who flee Florence to escape the Plague, in the Middle Ages, and then entertain themselves in a rural retreat with storytelling and music.

Boris was our Pied Piper, you might say! And the Lark Quartet was his best-known creation, his greatest achievement. Now it's gone. Does that matter? Do any of us matter? Victims of this Pestilence, this Plague, this COVID Pandemic?

Jennifer and I set off after lunching with Alice. We thanked her for her hospitality; "You're very welcome" she said. Then we ate in near-silence. Exhausted?

There was much less traffic on the highway to Hamilton than I had expected. At first Jennifer and I continued our silence. Then I asked her what her plans were.

"Well, I guess to go back to reality, whatever that is" she said. "I don't know if the University will function at all for a while – even small classes won't be allowed, and it looks as if all educational facilities will continue to be locked down, at least until COVID-19 is clearly under control, and who knows how long that will be?"

"You know you'd be very welcome to live with me in my house' I said. 'You'd be completely free to come and go, of course. We could work out a productive way of sharing shopping and the kitchen etcetera, and – well, I know we could work out everything amicably –"

"Oh, Anna, that's so good of you. Yes, I'd like that. I know we could work things out without any problems, as you say. And I have to work out my *future* too – once things are generally a bit clearer. I do have some savings, but I know my Cousin can help if necessary, he said to just – I'll call him tonight. Did I tell you he lives in Vancouver? Or did. I thought of going to live there, but I guess that wouldn't be sensible or even possible as things are."

'No, I think you're right. I wonder what changes are coming? Did I tell you that I was worried the Police might come after us, at Boris's house? We weren't wearing masks, and I think that's maybe required now in public; when shopping, or even walking? I'm sure that you and the others kept the right distance apart when you were out walking near the house. But I was mostly worried about the five of us – six of us, counting Alice – in the house. I didn't think about that at first, and of course we couldn't possibly have spread any infection beyond the house, if we'd had any to spread, but I think it was still disobeying rules – Well, you get so worried about unintentionally disobeying rules of behavior in this sort of situation; and being a cause of spreading that terrible virus? What do you think?"

"I must admit I didn't worry about any of that, but I'll have to now, won't I?"

And we arrived in Hamilton.

P.S.

And so: Life, as they say, Goes On – But the effects of the CO-VID-19 Plague will certainly be profound, reducing populations and economies, and causing major changes in daily life and behavior around the world; mainly negative changes, surely; at least until things settle down? And worst of all, some think (and I agree) that COVID-19 has distracted attention so profoundly from the ever-advancing threat of Global Warming, the general degradation of the world, and the widespread destruction of wild-life, that the future, even when the Plague does end, seems bleak indeed. – So, Boris, what do you say now? "The C Major of this life"? No? G Minor? And I am glad that I will probably follow you into the Darkness before long – before the next Plague arrives.

Monday 18th May

Gloomy morning! Light rain. Temperature (I think) about 11 degrees. We have decided to take a trip to the Butterfly Garden, on the edge of Dundas, and have a walk there before lunch. Somehow it has remained open while all other local parks and recreation-areas have been locked-down; but it seems that public Parks and maybe even camp-grounds may soon be open, by Ontario Govt decree. Our world is about to open up again – but with nervous concern about possible further outbreaks of "Covid" (as people are referring to it increasingly, I think: the past will be known as "Pre-Covid" and the future as "Post-Covid"?).

It's a holiday! VICTORIA DAY. I think Canada is the only country that still celebrates (with fireworks!) that sad monarch, who mourned the man she had adored, and lived on and on and on. But writing this reminds me to telephone dear Alice, for another bout of mutually-encouraging chat. Yes, as soon as I finish writing this Farewell!

Hard to know, or even guess, where we'll be (IF we'll be?) in even the near future: as Canadians, as North Americans, as human-beings. And will democracy survive? Unsatisfactory as it is, it's surely still "better than the alternative" (as Churchill claimed): better than a world cowed by aggressive nations ruled by rich bullies who, like Trump and fellow-autocrats, bash as "fake-news" any attempts at truth-telling, and who viciously exploit whole communities to increase their personal power and wealth. And will we, can we, find ways to end the despoiling of this beautiful Earth, before it's too late? And – So many worries beyond the horizon of our Plague. But I am merely an elderly woman On Her Way Out! Who writes, who chatters, who Repeats Herself, who is totally without influence! Oh, Alice, dear Alice, where art thou?

Thursday 28th May

Oh, a miserable day. Pouring rain. Grey, grey. Morning news: COVID-19 death-count in the United States of America: over 100,000: more than the total number of US deaths in Korea, Vietnam, etc. What about today's Canadian numbers? Do I really want to know? I have a vision of corpses piling up, piling up, as in those photos of Auschwitz that one struggles to forget.

But most immediately troubling news came in early-morning phone call from Ken. James in hospital with COVID and may not survive. "They won't let me see him, I begged them but–" Ken was crying, and now I am too. "I can't bear it" he said, over and over.

You can, Ken. You will, Ken. You must, Ken.